HOME-RUN HITTERS

HEROES OF THE
FOUR HOME-RUN GAME

BY JOHN A. TORRES

MACMILLAN BOOKS FOR YOUNG READERS • NEW YORK

6/95   15.00

Macmillan Books for Young Readers
An imprint of Simon & Schuster Children's Publishing Division
Simon & Schuster Macmillan
1230 Avenue of the Americas
New York, New York 10020

Designed by Joseph Rutt

Manufactured in the United States of America

First edition

10 9 8 7 6 5 4 3 2 1

Library of Congress Cataloging-in-Publication Data

Torres, John Albert.
    Home-run hitters ; heroes of the four home-run game / by John A.
Torres. — 1st ed.
        p.   cm.
    Includes bibliographical references and index.
    ISBN 0-02-789407-X
    1. Baseball players—United States—Biography—Juvenile
literature.   2. Home runs (Baseball)—Juvenile literature.
[1. Baseball players.   2. Home runs (Baseball)]   I. Title.
GV865.A1T675   1995
796.357'092—dc20
[B]   94-13554

To my wife, Julie, and my son, Daniel,
who, like the sun, fill my days with warmth,
inspiration, and a star to wish upon

Contents

Introduction

The confrontation between pitcher and batter is arguably the most intense individual matchup in sports. The flame-throwing pitcher hurling a baseball ninety miles an hour toward a lean slugger poised with his bat is as exciting a battle as any. The strikeout represents the ultimate victory for the pitcher, while the home run is a clear triumph for the hitter.

No other play in baseball sparks as much conversation and emotion as the home run. Home runs win pennants, make record books, and break hearts. There have been many great home-run hitters over the years. Some—Hank Aaron and Babe Ruth, for example—have been known for their staggering career totals. Others, such as Ralph Kiner, Roger Maris, Mickey Mantle, and Jimmy Foxx, have been known for their tremendous single-season totals. Still others have been known as "tape-measure" or "moon-shot" sluggers. Dave Kingman, Frank Howard, and Jose Canseco are familiar names of long-ball hitters. Some players, perhaps not known for being home-run hitters, will always be remembered for a particular home run.

Who doesn't associate the name Bobby Thomson with the "shot heard 'round the world"? Thomson will always be remembered for his dramatic ninth-inning home run for the New York Giants to win the 1951 National League playoffs against Ralph Branca and the Brooklyn Dodgers.

Bill Mazeroski of the Pittsburgh Pirates was a tremendous second baseman who played on seven all-star teams and won eight Gold Glove awards. Mazeroski is probably best remembered, though, for his ninth-inning home run in the seventh game of the 1960 World Series to defeat the New York Yankees.

Who can forget Bucky Dent driving a stake through the hearts of Red Sox fans everywhere with his improbable three-run home run during a one-game playoff in 1978? His Yankees team, perhaps inspired by that unexpected home run, went on to win the World Series.

The pitch is thrown. With the crack of the bat, fans jump to their feet to watch the outfielder desperately trying to catch the ball as it sails over the fence. The home run can stir up a lackluster crowd or immediately silence the fans in the stands. Home runs help create heroes; two-homer games create superstars; three-homer games create legends. But four home runs in one game?

The odds against this phenomenal display of power are mind-boggling. Everything needs to fall perfectly into place.

First, the batter needs four chances at the plate. Second, he must rely on a perfect home-run stroke and solid contact when he swings. Third, the slugger must get a pitch that he can drive out of the park.

Since 1900, only ten baseball players have connected to hit four home runs in one game. These sluggers all possessed great strength and the ability to hit home runs in bunches. And, as at least one of them acknowledged, they all had a lucky day at the plate.

The following chapters will take an intimate look at the players in the "Four" club and help relive their careers, their ups and downs, and, of course, their home runs.

CHAPTER ONE

Premodern Era to Babe Ruth

Baseball history, as well as its record books, is broken up into two distinct time periods: The premodern baseball era and the modern baseball era. The premodern era is baseball before 1900. The modern era began then and continues today.

In the premodern era the rules were basically the same as they are in the 1990s (although walks and errors sometimes counted as hits), but there were a lot of fundamental differences in the overall game.

There were no indoor stadiums or artificial-turf fields. There was no such thing as free agency, and there were hardly any trades (most players were simply sold from team to team). The ball was heavier than it is today, and the gloves were a lot smaller. Pitchers did not throw as fast as they can today, but spitballs were legal.

Most of all, the attitude of the player was different. Ballplayers played baseball simply because they loved the game. Believe it or not, ballplayers made little money, and many of the players held second jobs.

The strategy during the premodern era was basically to try to score one run at a time. Teams would scratch and claw to try to manufacture a run. A typical scoring rally would go something like this: A batter reaches first base via a walk or a hit. He is then moved to second base by a sacrifice bunt, hit-and-run play, or stolen base. From second he could score on a base hit to the outfield or could advance to third on a well-placed ground out. With fewer than two outs, a runner could score from third base on an out.

Home runs were a scarce commodity during the premodern era, and the power hitter was not yet recognized as an offensive force. Even so, two players of the premodern era accomplished the phenomenal feat of hitting four home runs in a single game.

The first player ever to do it was Robert Lincoln "Bobby" Lowe. Bobby was a right-handed leadoff hitter who was known more for his slick fielding than for his batting. He played second base for the Boston Beaneaters (who later became the Braves) from 1890 to 1901 on what was known as a great defensive infield. Lowe's steady play at second and his spunkiness as the leadoff hitter helped Boston win five pennants during the 1890s.

Lowe made it into the record books on May 30, 1894, when he became the first player to belt four home runs in one game. All four dingers were hit off of Cincinnati's Elton "Iceberg" Chamberlain. They were all hit from the relatively close distance of 250 feet over the left-field wall of Boston's

Congress Street Grounds. Boston's regular ballpark was being renovated at the time. The Beaneaters won the game 20–11. The fans showered the 150-pound Lowe with silver coins after the contest.

Lowe finished his eighteen-year, four-team career with a .273 batting average and 70 home runs.

The second man to hit four round-trippers in a game was Edward "Big Ed" Delahanty. Active from 1888 to 1903, Big Ed was one of five Delahanty brothers to play in the major leagues. The six-foot–one-inch right-hander from Cleveland, Ohio, was a consistent contact hitter. He led both leagues in batting, and his career batting average of .346, including three .400 seasons, is fifth-best of all time. He led the National League in home runs one season and in runs batted in (RBIs) three seasons. On July 13, 1896, he smashed four homers and a single as his Philadelphia Phillies lost to Chicago. Big Ed was voted into the Baseball Hall of Fame in 1945.

Although the record books are separated by the turn of the century, the game did not change much during the early 1900s. The home run was still a rarity, and consistent hitting was more valued than power. For example, Frank "Home Run" Baker led the American League in homers for four consecutive seasons, although his highest single-season total was twelve. Ty Cobb once led the league with a mere nine home runs.

In 1919, baseball suffered through its darkest hour with the infamous Black Sox scandal. Eight players from the American League–Champion Chicago White Sox were found guilty of losing the World Series for money. Baseball's image was tainted and fans everywhere were searching for a hero. A year later they found him. His name was Babe Ruth.

It was not until Babe began smashing homers for the Red Sox and then the Yankees that the home run became the offensive weapon that it is today. Ruth's gargantuan size, massive home runs, and charisma made him a fan favorite. His visits to sick and needy children made him an idol to children everywhere.

Babe Ruth started his career as a pitcher, but his strong bat convinced the Red Sox that he should play every day. He responded by setting a major-league record with 29 home runs in 1919 for Boston. (The American League record had been 16 homers.) After being sold to the Yankees in time for the 1920 season, Ruth broke his own record with 54 round-trippers and became America's most famous baseball player. The fans were coming in droves just to see Babe take his cuts. The Yankees set a record in 1920 by drawing 1,289,422 fans.

Babe kept improving his own record when he hit 59 homers in 1921 and then 60 in 1927 as part of the famous Murderers' Row Yankees' lineup, which boasted several home-run hitters, including Lou Gehrig.

Ruth's lore is not confined to statistics or tape-measure home runs. His antics, his feats, and his charitable manner made him a player of legendary proportions. From his promising sick children home runs, to his famous "called shot" during the 1932 World Series (when Ruth supposedly pointed to a spot in the bleachers where he then hit the next pitch), the legend of the Babe grew. Babe Ruth gave the Yankees the edge they needed. He turned them from a team on the rise to a World Series mainstay.

Thanks to Ruth's popularity, the home run and the home run hitter flourished.

Today's slugger still commands attention when he steps into the batter's box. Every spectator seems to sense that one swing of the bat can turn the game around, change the course of the season, or even make history.

CHAPTER TWO

Lou Gehrig

It was a July fourth to be remembered: one filled with happiness and appreciation and sadness. Yankee Stadium was packed that Wednesday afternoon in 1939 as eager baseball fans listened intently to a very ill Lou Gehrig describe what it was like to have been a New York Yankee.

"You've been reading about my bad break for weeks now. But today, I consider myself the luckiest man on the face of the earth," a tearful Gehrig said as 61,808 fans rose to acknowledge one of the best ballplayers ever.

Lou's awesome reputation as one of the all-time greats has stood the test of time. The Iron Horse, as he was affectionately called, holds the record for most consecutive appearances. Never having missed a game in over thirteen seasons, he played in an astonishing 2,130 games. A smooth-fielding first baseman, Gehrig was one of the mainstays of the Yankees' lineup, along with Babe Ruth. He pounded 493 home runs, drove in 1,991 runs, and collected 2,721 hits while averaging .340 for his career.

Louis Henry Gehrig was born Ludwig Heinrich Gehrig to German-American parents on June 19, 1903, in New York City. He grew up in the predominantly German neighborhood of Yorkville and did not learn how to speak English until he was sent to kindergarten at the age of five.

Right from his childhood, it seemed that Gehrig was destined for greatness. By the time he was eleven years old, he'd been a star on his school track team and led his parks-department baseball team to the city championship. Yet Gehrig suffered greatly from shyness.

He refused to join his high school baseball team because of his fear of playing in front of large crowds. However, the baseball coach, Du Schatko, was persistent. He gave Lou a uniform and ordered him to report to the team. Gehrig was tried in the outfield but was too clumsy. He was put in to pitch but was too wild. Finally he was put at first base, which he would call home for years to come.

Although Lou batted under .200 during his three years of high school, his love of sports grew. He joined the school's soccer team as well as the football team.

At Columbia University in New York, Lou played right tackle for the football team and soon began whacking baseballs as Columbia's regular first baseman.

Gehrig began to make a name for himself on the diamond, becoming a star on the Columbia Lions. His hitting prowess attracted scouts from the major leagues. The hometown Yankees were particularly interested. The story goes that the Yankees paid five hundred dollars to Columbia baseball coach Andy Coakley, an ex–major leaguer himself, to talk Gehrig into signing a contract with them.

Gehrig signed and played two seasons with the Yankees' minor Eastern League farm team in Hartford, Connecticut. He played a steady first base and consistently drove the ball to all parts of the field. Just four days short of his twentieth birthday, Gehrig was called up to the majors.

Lou was used primarily as a pinch hitter, and it was not until June 1, 1925, when New York's starting first baseman, Wally Pipp, sat out a game with a headache that Lou finally had a chance to play. He never stopped. From that moment, Gehrig was a regular.

The left-handed slugger had an incredible rookie season. He belted 20 home runs, drove in 68 runs, and batted .295. In two short years Gehrig was made the Yankees' cleanup hitter and batted between future Hall of Famer Babe Ruth and slugger Bob Meusel. In 1927, the Yankees' lineup became known as Murderers' Row. That year Gehrig put up numbers that were truly astounding. He cracked 47 home runs and drove in an unbelievable 175 runs while batting .373 to lead the dominating Yankees to a World Series crown. Lou was awarded the American League's Most Valuable Player award for the season and probably would have won it a few more times, but in those days a player could only win the award once.

While he was the starting first baseman, Lou and the rest of Murderers' Row appeared in seven World Series between 1926 and 1938, winning six of them. Lou drove in runs in record numbers for the "Bronx Bombers," hitting 174 RBIs in 1930, with 41 home runs and a .379 batting average, and followed that up in 1931 with a career-high 184 RBIs and 46 home runs. Never before had a team been so dominant in back-to-back seasons.

Gehrig and Ruth were the two most prolific home run hitters ever to bat one after the other, and often competed for the season's home run crown. Their personalities were such opposites that Gehrig's quiet, steady shyness and the Babe's loud, outlandish ways were often misread as proof that they disliked each other. This is not true. They were merely different.

Although Ruth was the more famous of the two home run hitters and reigned as the all-time home run champion for 39 years, Lou accomplished something the Babe never did.

On June 3, 1932, Lou became the first player in the twentieth century to swat four home runs in one game, leading the visiting Yankees to a 20–13 victory over the Philadelphia Athletics in a homer fest. The Yankees clouted seven home runs to tie the record for most homers by a team in one game.

Lou smashed home runs his first four times at the plate. He had a two-run homer in the first inning, and his next three were solo shots. The crowd of five thousand spectators buzzed in anticipation, encouraging Gehrig to hit a fifth. He had two chances, but he grounded out in the eighth and flew out in the ninth. Ironically, his hardest shot of the day was the fly-out in the ninth; Philadelphia outfielder Al Simmons made a leaping catch at the wall, snaring what looked like a potential fifth homer.

Shibe Park, in Philadelphia, was always known as a very hard park to hit home runs in. Players often referred to it as cavernous. Yet the powerful Gehrig had no problem sending four balls, and nearly a fifth one, over its fence.

After the ball game, Lou's teammates teased the Iron Horse

about losing too many balls with his home runs. "You're costing the American League too much money," they kidded.

Lou, avoiding the spotlight as always, hugged Babe Ruth after the game and said, "I did it for us." By this time the Babe was thirty-seven years old, and his great career was coming to an end.

Lou continued to dominate the game for the next six years, batting in more than 113 runs each season and hitting better than .300 for five of the six years. He was chosen to the American League all-star team all six years as well.

Lou's standards were so high that he spoke of retirement after what he considered to be an "off" season in 1938. He had batted .295 with 29 home runs and 114 runs batted in—some off season! Still, he felt as if he had slowed down a step and wondered if his skills were diminishing. Lou reported to spring training in 1939 and decided to give it another year; after all, he had not missed a game since 1925.

Lou started the season slowly, and it was evident that he had lost a step. Sporting a sub-.200 batting average a full month into the season, Gehrig went to see Yankees manager Joe McCarthy.

"I'm playing terribly right now, Joe. I'm not helping the team at all. I want you to take me out," Lou said.

That afternoon, May 2, 1939, 2,130 games after his Iron Horse legacy had begun, Gehrig handed a lineup card—without his name on it—to the umpire. It was reported that Gehrig had tears in his eyes.

Lou was puzzled by his decline and decided to go to the doctor. On June 21, 1939, Lou and his doctor announced that he was suffering from amyotrophic lateral sclerosis, an incurable muscle disease.

The Yankees honored the great Lou Gehrig on July 4, 1939. Most of his 1927 Murderers' Row teammates were on hand to honor him and encourage him in his fight against the debilitating disease that was slowly taking his life. They all paraded onto the diamond, perhaps the greatest team to ever grace the playing field: Babe Ruth, Bob Meusel, Waite Hoyt, Tony Lazzeri, Mark Koenig, Joe Dugan, Bob Shawkey, Herb Pennock, Everett Scott, Wally Pipp, Wally Schang, and Benny Bengough.

In accepting the gifts from former teammates and the undying admiration from his many fans, Gehrig paid homage to the Yankees legends standing beside him. "What young man wouldn't give anything to mingle with such men for a single day as I have all these years?" he asked.

Lou was inducted into the Baseball Hall of Fame in 1939. The mandatory five-year waiting period for retired ballplayers had been waived due to the gravity of his illness.

Gehrig took a job with the New York City Parole Commission Offices and worked there until his death on June 2, 1941.

The baseball world was shocked at the Iron Horse's sudden decline and quick death.

A poem was composed by *New York Times* writer John Kieran and was engraved on a silver trophy that had been presented to Lou during his tribute. It read:

> We've been to the wars together,
> we took our foes as they came;
> and always you were the leader,
> and ever you played the game.

Idol of cheering millions;
records are yours by sheaves;
Iron of frame they hailed you,
decked you with laurel leaves.

But higher than that we hold you,
we who have known you best;
knowing the way you came through
every human test.

Let this be a silent token
of lasting friendship's gleam
and all that we've left unspoken
—your pals on the Yankee team.

Gehrig, Louis Henry (The Iron Horse, Columbia Lou)

Born Ludwig Heinrich Gehrig.
b. June 19, 1903, New York, N.Y.   d. June 2, 1941, New York, N.Y.
Hall of Fame 1939.

YEAR	TEAM	GAMES	BA	SA	AB	H	2B	3B
1923	NY A	13	.423	.769	26	11	4	1
1924		10	.500	.583	12	6	1	0
1925		126	.295	.531	437	129	23	10
1926		155	.313	.549	572	179	47	20
1927		155	.373	.765	584	218	52	18
1928		154	.374	.648	562	210	47	13
1929		154	.300	.582	553	166	33	9
1930		154	.379	.721	581	220	42	17
1931		155	.341	.662	619	211	31	15
1932		156	.349	.621	596	208	42	9
1933		152	.334	.605	593	198	41	12
1934		154	.363	.706	579	210	40	6
1935		149	.329	.583	535	176	26	10
1936		155	.354	.696	579	205	37	7
1937		157	.351	.643	569	200	37	9
1938		157	.295	.523	576	170	32	6
1939		8	.143	.143	28	4	0	0
17 yrs.		2164	.340	.632 3rd	8001	2721	535	162

WORLD SERIES

YEAR	TEAM	GAMES	BA	SA	AB	H	2B	3B
1926	NY A	7	.348	.435	23	8	2	0
1927		4	.308	.769	13	4	2	2
1928		4	.545	1.727	11	6	1	0
1932		4	.529	1.118	17	9	1	0
1936		6	.292	.583	24	7	1	0
1937		5	.294	.647	17	5	1	1
1938		4	.286	.286	14	4	0	0
7 yrs.		34	.361	.731	119	43	8	3

YEAR	HR	HR%	R	RBI	BB	SO	SB
1923	1	3.8	6	9	2	5	0
1924	0	0.0	2	5	1	3	0
1925	20	4.6	73	68	46	49	6
1926	16	2.8	135	107	105	72	6
1927	47	8.0	149	175	109	84	10
1928	27	4.8	139	142	95	69	4
1929	35	6.3	127	126	122	68	4
1930	41	7.1	143	174	101	63	12
1931	46	7.4	163	184	117	56	17
1932	34	5.7	138	151	108	38	4
1933	32	5.4	138	139	92	42	9
1934	49	8.5	128	165	109	31	9
1935	30	5.6	125	119	132	38	8
1936	49	8.5	167	152	130	46	3
1937	37	6.5	138	159	127	49	4
1938	29	5.0	115	114	107	75	6
1939	0	0.0	2	1	5	1	0
17 yrs.	493	6.2	1888	1990	1508	789	102
			7th	3rd			
WORLD SERIES							
1926	0	0.0	1	3	5	4	0
1927	0	0.0	2	5	3	3	0
1928	4	36.4	5	9	6	0	0
1932	3	17.6	9	8	2	1	0
1936	2	8.3	5	7	3	2	0
1937	1	5.9	4	3	5	4	0
1938	0	0.0	4	0	2	3	0
7 yrs.	10	8.4	30	35	26	17	0

CHAPTER THREE

Chuck Klein

Hall of Fame right fielder Chuck Klein was almost a member of the New York Yankees Murderers' Row. But the Yankees did not exercise their option on Klein, and the Philadelphia Phillies purchased his contract for five thousand dollars.

It was money well spent!

Chuck Klein went on to hit 300 homers and compile a .320 batting average during a seventeen-year career. Chuck established many records that have stood the test of time. He still holds the National League single-season marks for total bases by a left-handed hitter (445), most runs batted in by a left-hander (170), most long hits by a left-handed batter (107), and most games with one or more hits (135).

Chuck was born October 7, 1904, in Indianapolis, Indiana.

Described as a big, gawky kid, Klein stood six feet and weighed 185 pounds. After attending Southport High School, Chuck began working for a construction road gang. Later, he built up his strength by hurling two-hundred-pound ingots around a steel mill. Chuck was an accomplished steelworker by the time he signed his first professional baseball contract in 1927.

He was twenty-one years old when he signed with Evansville of the Three I League. Chuck was switched back and forth between right field and first base. He batted .327 over fourteen games and was promoted to Fort Wayne of the Central League. He tore up the Central League with a .331 average and 26 home runs. Then the Phillies purchased his contract, and he was called up late in July.

Chuck entered the major leagues after playing in only 102 minor league games. The Phillies were then well on their way to a third consecutive last-place finish. Phillies manager Burt Shotton took a look at Klein and said, "They tell me you can hit. Goodness knows, we need hitters."

Klein popped out as a pinch hitter during his first major-league at bat, but the next day he smashed a home run and a double. He finished his rookie campaign with 11 homers and a .360 average.

During the next five seasons, Chuck made baseball history. He assembled the five greatest years that any National League power hitter has ever had. Many players who do well in their rookie season put too much pressure on themselves to do better the next year. Many times this extra pressure causes the young player to have a bad second season. This is known as the sophomore jinx. Klein scoffed at the jinx by batting .356, hitting 43 home runs and 45 doubles, and driving in 145 runs while scoring 126. His 43 home runs led the league that year and established a Phillies record that stood until Mike Schmidt belted 48 homers in 1980.

Critics pointed out that the right-field fence at Philadelphia's home park, the Baker Bowl, was only 280 feet away from home plate. Chuck responded by saying, "I also slammed a lot of drives off that fence that would have been home runs in bigger parks." The right-field fence in Philadelphia was forty-five feet high. As if to drive home his point, Klein hit a home run in every opposing ballpark that season.

The following season, 1930, was filled with amazing statistics and ironies for Klein and the Phillies. Philadelphia batted .315 as a team for the season, yet finished last, forty games out of first, with a record of 52–102. The league batting average that season was .303. Klein led Philadelphia's batting onslaught by putting together his finest season.

Although Chuck's batting statistics were outstanding, he did not lead the league in many of the major offensive categories. New York Giants first baseman Bill Terry led the league with a .401 batting average and 254 hits, while Chicago Cubs center fielder Hack Wilson established the still-standing National League records of 56 home runs and 190 RBIs.

Chuck did have something to show for his amazing season, though, by leading the league in doubles, runs scored, total bases, and a defensive record—which stands today—of 44 outfield assists.

Chuck's batting feats were breaking more than records. His

home runs were a menace to the passing traffic on Broad Street, just outside the Baker Bowl. Numerous car windshields were broken by Chuck's home runs. Phillies owner William Baker had a policy of paying for the broken windshields. Before Baker died in 1930, he tried to curtail the staggering home run totals by adding a fifteen-foot-high screen to the top of the right field fence, making it sixty feet high.

Baker said, "Home runs have become too cheap at the Philadelphia ball park." However, most people speculated that Baker was trying to keep Klein from reaching Babe Ruth's home run totals so that he would not have to pay Klein a salary comparable to Ruth's.

During this period Klein was gaining a reputation for being one of baseball's hardest-working players. The fans loved his hustling and his never-say-die attitude. He was known for always playing as if the game were on the line, no matter the score or the inning. *The Phillies' Encyclopedia* described Klein as "a conscientious worker who hustled all the time."

In the 1931 season, Chuck batted .337 with 31 homers and 121 runs batted in. It was in 1932, however, that Klein finally led the Phillies out of last place. Chuck was voted the league's Most Valuable Player as he led the league in hits, runs, stolen bases, total bases, and slugging average (percentage). He tied for the lead in home runs. Philadelphia finished in fourth place, their highest standing since 1917.

In 1933 Klein capped his incredible five-year hitting spree by winning the National League's Triple Crown, which is awarded when a player leads the league in batting average, home runs, and RBIs. There have been only five Triple Crown winners in the National League since 1900. During his five-year batting rampage Klein averaged .359, 36 home runs, and 139 runs batted in per season.

By November 1933, the Phillies were struggling financially to keep the franchise afloat. The fans were tiring of a team that had topped the .500 mark only once since 1917. The Phillies had finished last eight times in the previous fifteen years. The Baker Bowl, which seated about 18,000 fans, was looking emptier and emptier every year. The team's new owner, Gary Nugent, was in constant financial trouble, so he sold or traded most of the team's best players. The Phillies traded Klein to the Chicago Cubs for three mediocre players and $65,000.

Klein played well with Chicago but never enjoyed the kind of success he had while hitting in the friendly confines of the Baker Bowl. In his first game against his old teammates, Klein rose to the occasion, smashing two home runs, leading the Cubs to a 10–3 victory. Chuck's .293 batting average and 21 home runs in 1935 helped the Chicago Cubs win the National League pennant. Even though Chuck batted .333 with a two-run homer, the Cubs lost the World Series to the Detroit Tigers four games to two.

Klein was traded back to Philadelphia in May 1936 for what would turn out to be his last great season. That season, Klein became the first National League player, in the modern era, to hit four home runs in a single game.

On July 10, Klein led the visiting Phillies to a 9–6 ten-inning victory over the Pittsburgh Pirates. Chuck smashed a three-run shot in the first inning against fork-ball pitcher "Big Jim" Weaver, a solo home run against Weaver in the fifth, another solo home run against Mace Brown in the seventh, and the game winner against Bill Swift to lead off the tenth. The Phillies tacked on two more runs against Swift after the home run. Although the game was on the line, the Pittsburgh fans were standing and cheering as Klein strode to the plate to lead off the tenth. The left-handed slugger swung and took Swift's fastball deep to right field. The fans, players, and Klein knew the ball was out of the ballpark the instant he swung the bat. But soft-spoken Klein simply circled the bases as if it were any other home run.

Chuck was responsible for driving in six of Philadelphia's nine runs that day. He nearly hit a fifth home run with a second-inning drive that was pulled down by Paul Waner with his back to the right-field fence.

Chuck raised his average to .325 in 1937 but, for the first time since 1928, did not reach the twenty home-run plateau. By 1938, Klein's skills were clearly diminishing, and he was released by the Phillies early in the 1939 season. He was signed by the Pirates and batted .300 for them, but was released after the season.

Chuck joined the Phillies for a third stint in the spring of 1940 and was the starting right fielder. He managed only seven home runs in the newly built, spacious Shibe Park; his batting average dipped to .218. Chuck became a player-coach for the Phillies in 1941, filling in as a pinch hitter or extra outfielder until his retirement in 1944.

Chuck operated his own business in Philadelphia until 1947, when he became very ill. The great player never recovered. He died from a brain hemorrhage in 1958.

In 1980, baseball's Hall of Fame Veterans' Committee gave

one of baseball's outstanding hitters his due when they elected Klein to the Hall of Fame.

"It took only two players like Chuck Klein to make a winning team," wrote the *New York Times* at the time of Chuck's death. "Unfortunately, the Phillies only had one."

Klein, Charles Herbert

b. Oct. 7, 1904, Indianapolis, Ind. d. Mar. 28, 1958, Indianapolis, Ind.
Hall of Fame 1980.

YEAR TEAM	GAMES	BA	SA	AB	H	2B	3B
1928 PHI N	64	.360	.577	253	91	14	4
1929	149	.356	.657	616	219	45	6
1930	156	.386	.687	648	250	59	8
1931	148	.337	.584	594	200	34	10
1932	154	.348	.646	650	226	50	15
1933	152	.368	.602	606	223	44	7
1934 CHI N	115	.301	.510	435	131	27	2
1935	119	.293	.488	434	127	14	4
1936 2 teams CHI N (29G——.294) PHI N (117G——.309)							
" total	146	.306	.512	601	184	35	7
1937 PHI N	115	.325	.495	406	132	20	2
1938	129	.247	.356	458	113	22	2
1939 2 teams PHI N (25G——.191) PIT N (85G——. 300)							
" total	110	.284	.486	317	90	18	5
1940 PHI N	116	.218	.333	354	77	16	2
1941	50	.123	.164	73	9	0	0
1942	14	.071	.071	14	1	0	0
1943	12	.100	.100	20	2	0	0
1944	4	.143	.143	7	1	0	0
17 yrs.	1753	.320	.543	6486	2076	398	74

WORLD SERIES

YEAR TEAM	GAMES	BA	SA	AB	H	2B	3B
1935 CHI N	5	.333	.583	12	4	0	0

YEAR	HR	HR%	R	RBI	BB	SO	SB
1928	11	4.3	41	34	14	22	0
1929	43	7.0	126	145	54	61	5
1930	40	6.2	158	170	54	50	4
1931	31	5.2	121	121	59	49	7
1932	38	5.8	152	137	60	49	20
1933	28	4.6	101	120	56	36	15
1934	20	4.6	78	80	47	38	3
1935	21	4.8	71	73	41	42	4
1936							
"	25	4.2	102	105	49	59	6
1937	15	3.7	74	57	39	21	3
1938	8	1.7	53	61	38	30	7
1939							
"	12	3.8	45	56	36	21	2
1940	7	2.0	39	37	44	30	2
1941	1	1.4	6	3	10	6	0
1942	0	0.0	0	0	0	2	0
1943	0	0.0	0	3	0	3	1
1944	0	0.0	1	0	0	2	0
17 yrs.	300	4.6	1168	1202	601	521	79

WORLD SERIES

YEAR	HR	HR%	R	RBI	BB	SO	SB
1935	1	8.3	2	2	0	2	0

CHAPTER FOUR

Pat Seerey

⚾

"Curveballitis." It is a common affliction that ends many major-league baseball careers. Curveball after curveball dies on the outside part of home plate, tempting young sluggers to swing, lunge, hack, and often to miss.

James Patrick Seerey hit only eighty-six home runs during his seven-year major-league career, and he led the American League in striking out for four of those seven seasons. The big, burly Seerey was a fan favorite known for his wild swings and his feast-or-famine approach to hitting. He was a frequent victim of curveballitis.

Pat was always big and powerful for his age. He was born on Saint Patrick's Day, March 17, 1923, to Irish-American parents in Wilburton, Oklahoma. His father was a railroad worker who moved his family to Arkansas when Pat was six months old. As he grew up in Little Rock, Pat became involved in sports.

Pat always batted cleanup when he played American Legion baseball and fullback when he played football. His lack of speed ruled out a possible college football scholarship, and his knack for hitting tape-measure home runs kept his focus on playing baseball.

"Sure, I played football," Pat said. "That was at Catholic High School in Little Rock. We had only 185 kids in the school. For four years I was the big, crashing fullback. And we always seemed to be getting our ears beaten off. I wasn't a speed demon but I'm not as slow as you might think. Funny though, I play center field in baseball."

Center fielders are usually not built like "big, crashing fullbacks." Center fielders are usually the fastest and most graceful players on the team because they have to cover the most ground. The center-field fence is always the farthest away from home plate, and the center fielder has to patrol the gaps as well as back up the right and left fielders.

Seerey played an excellent center field and was soon noticed by Cleveland Indians scout Harold Irelan. He signed Pat to a minor-league contract with Appleton of the Wisconsin State League in 1941 after Pat graduated from high school. Pat did not disappoint anyone. He batted .330, smashed 31 home runs, and drove 135 runs across the plate, giving Cleveland fans hope for the future.

Irelan was impressed. "Watch that boy, Seerey," he told reporters. "He's not going to be a good hitter. He's going to be one of the best of all time."

Pat was promoted to Cedar Rapids, Iowa, where he batted .301 with 33 homers and 92 runs batted in. In 1943 he began the season one step closer to the major leagues at Wilkes-Barre, Pennsylvania, going hitless in twelve consecutive games. He carried a pitiful .045 average six weeks into the season. Then Seerey got hot, and the Indians, desperate because several of their players were serving in World War II, called him up to the majors on June 9.

A starry-eyed Pat admitted being a bit nervous about the promotion. "I never saw a major-league park in my life until I joined the Indians. The stadium looked as big as a cow pasture in Arkansas," he said.

Lou Boudreau, Cleveland's manager, liked Pat's size and his minor-league numbers. Pat immediately became the right-handed half of a left-field platoon with Jeff Heath. A platoon in baseball is when two players share a position. Usually it involves a right-handed hitter and a left-handed hitter. The right-hander plays whenever the opposing team starts a lefty pitcher, and the left-handed hitter starts against right-handed pitchers. Platoons are very often successful with young ballplayers, helping them establish confidence in themselves while not having to face the pitchers that give them the most trouble. Seerey played hard his first year, but struggled with his weight and managed only 1 home run in twenty-six games.

The five-foot–ten-inch Seerey weighed 228 pounds during his rookie season. He looked much more like a thick-necked football player than a fleet-footed left fielder. He worked hard during the off-season and reported in much better shape for the 1944 campaign.

Pat started 86 games in the outfield and hit 15 home runs with 39 RBIs. But he still showed little patience with the curveball, striking out a league-leading ninety-nine times.

"Pat Seerey is an utter and complete sucker for the curveball on the outside part of the plate," wrote Cleveland sportswriter Gordon Cobbledick. "He's never going to get anything but hooks [curveballs] to hit so he might as well get to cuttin' and slashin' at them."

Pat's failures at the plate began to follow him onto the field. He began turning routine plays into misadventures in the outfield. Although not charged with many errors, Pat was making routine fly balls into doubles and making circus catches.

The next season Pat managed 14 home runs but led the American League in strikeouts again by fanning 97 times. Even so, 1945 was the year that Pat showed his home-run explosiveness when he had the best day he ever had in the majors.

Pat blasted three home runs and a triple against the hometown New York Yankees as Cleveland walloped the Yanks 16–4 on July 13, 1945.

Pat drove in eight runs that day with a grand slam, a three-run shot, and a solo home run. He nearly had a fourth, but his line drive to left field caromed off the fence for a triple. The small Yankee Stadium crowd of 10,281 cheered and encouraged Pat as he took his hacks in the ninth inning. The gentle giant lined out to left field, ending his bid for a fourth home run.

"Believe it or not, that game against the Yankees was my best game," Seerey told the *St. Louis Post-Dispatch* in 1979. "I'll always remember the four homer day but that was my second-best game. The triple I hit was probably the hardest ball I hit all game. It just didn't get up. It was a line shot into the left-center field slot. I'll never forget the next game, either," Seerey recalled with a laugh. "My first time up they hit me in the middle of my back with the first pitch."

Pat's teammate, pitcher Bob Feller, admired Seerey's strength. "Pat hits balls farther than anybody I've ever seen," he said. "He's nowhere near the hitter [Ted] Williams is, for example, but he'll hit a ball farther."

In 1946 Seerey hit a career high of 26 home runs, but the Cleveland Indians were losing patience as Seerey struck out 101 times in 404 at bats and saw his average plummet to .225. Cleveland owner Bill Veeck hired one of baseball's greatest hitters, Hall of Famer Rogers Hornsby, to give an eight-week-long hitting school prior to spring training in 1947. The main objective of the camp was to cut down on Pat's strikeouts and increase his home run output. Hornsby found many flaws with Seerey's approach at the plate.

"The way we worked it out," Hornsby explained, "was to have Pat straighten up a bit, cut down his stride a trifle, and step less toward third base. But the main thing is that he hasn't been keeping his eye on the ball. Pat has a tendency to swing where he thinks the ball will be and not where it is."

Pat listened intently during the eight-week course and worked hard at correcting his flaws. It paid off on opening day of 1947 when Pat slapped a single and a double. There was just one problem: No matter what approach or batting stance Seerey used, he still suffered from curveballitis.

By midseason Cleveland manager Lou Boudreau lost his patience and benched the troubled slugger for the remainder of the year, using Seerey only for occasional starts and for pinch-hitting duty. On June 2, 1948, Pat was traded to the Chicago White Sox.

A few weeks later, on July 18, Pat joined baseball's immortals. He became the fifth player to hit four home runs in a game, and the visiting White Sox outslugged the Philadelphia Athletics 12–11 during the first game of a doubleheader.

Seerey's home runs provided Chicago baseball fans with a much-needed lift. Both Chicago's teams, the Cubs of the National League and Pat's White Sox, were mired in last place, with little hope in sight.

After striking out on his old nemesis, the curveball, in the first inning, Pat overcame curveballitis and connected on a curve for a solo home run against Carl Scheib in the fourth. He victimized a Scheib fastball for a two-run shot in the fifth. Pat then belted a three-run homer against reliever Bob Savage in the sixth before breaking an 11–11 deadlock in the top of the eleventh inning with a long home run against Lou Brissie. Two of his home runs were so monstrous that they landed on the roof of the stadium! By the end of the game, Seerey even had the 17,296 Philadelphia fans cheering his awesome power.

Pat's uncanny display also proved to be financially rewarding. A Philadelphia advertiser, Weather King Batteries, was offering a five-hundred-dollar prize to any player who hit four home runs in a game. Pat posed for photographers after the game, kissing his "lucky" bat and laughing about the bonus, which he received the next day. Chicago fans flooded local radio stations with calls to make sure Pat received his money.

Bobby Lowe, the first player to ever hit four homers in a game, back in 1894, was impressed with Seerey's size. "They tell me he's a big fellow," the eighty-year-old Lowe said. "He weighs more than two hundred pounds! Why that would almost make two of me."

After Pat's brief moment of glory, he continued to struggle at the plate. He finished the season with only average numbers. He also had 102 K's, leading the American League in strikeouts for a fourth time. Pat was released during the 1949 season and retired permanently from baseball at the tender age of twenty-six. It was an abrupt end to a career that was once so full of promise.

Pat moved his family to St. Louis and expressed little regret about his baseball career, except maybe about parting from the Cleveland Indians in 1948. "Naturally, I was sorry to leave the team," he would later say. "I regret never playing in the World Series with those guys." The 1948 Indians had gone on to win the World Series.

Pat got a job as a maintenance worker for the St. Louis Board of Education, and he and his wife raised four children. His oldest son, Mike, was an all-American soccer player for St. Louis University and went on to play in the Olympics and for the North American Soccer League.

Pat admitted during the early 1980s that he had stopped following baseball. "Baseball is so slow now. Three hours for a game? There has to be something wrong somewhere," he said. When asked about his four home-run game, Seerey laughed. "Anybody that hits four home runs in a game just has to be lucky. That's all."

Seerey, James Patrick

b. Mar. 17, 1923, Wilburton, Okla. d. Apr. 28, 1986, Jennings, Mo.

YEAR TEAM	GAMES	BA	SA	AB	H	2B	3B
1943 CLE A	26	.222	.306	72	16	3	0
1944	101	.232	.412	342	80	16	0
1945	126	.237	.401	414	98	22	2
1946	117	.225	.470	404	91	17	2
1947	82	.171	.352	216	37	4	1
1948 2 teams CLE A (10G—.261) CHI A (95G—.229)							
" total	105	.231	.419	363	84	11	0
1949 CHI A	4	.000	.000	4	0	0	0
7 yrs.	561	.224	.412	1815	406	73	5

YEAR	HR	HR%	R	RBI	BB	SO	SB
1943	1	1.4	8	5	4	19	0
1944	15	4.4	39	39	19	99	0
1945	14	3.4	56	56	66	97	1
1946	26	6.4	57	62	65	101	2
1947	11	5.1	24	29	34	66	0
1948 "	19	5.2	51	70	90	102	0
1949	0	0.0	1	0	3	1	0
7 yrs.	86	4.7	236	261	281	485	3

CHAPTER FIVE

Gil Hodges

As a youngster, Gilbert Ray Hodges dreamed of coaching baseball or basketball, so it was not surprising that he turned down a minor-league baseball contract to be a college baseball coach. It is also not surprising that Hodges became known as the Miracle Worker for turning the last-place New York Mets into the 1969 World Champions.

Not only was Gil Hodges a great manager during his brief coaching career, but he was also one of the most feared sluggers of his time. Hodges cracked 370 home runs and drove in 1,274 runs for the Brooklyn and Los Angeles Dodgers and the New York Mets. He smashed five World Series homers and played on seven all-star teams.

Gil Hodges was sometimes called Brooklyn's Lou Gehrig. He played the game with the same quiet determination. Perhaps Gil's main attribute, like Gehrig's, was his consistency. He provided the Dodgers with a graceful, steady first baseman, winning Gold Glove awards from 1957 to 1959. He also provided a home run bat in the Brooklyn lineup. Gil belted 20 or more home runs a year for eleven straight years.

What also made Gil a real fan favorite was his modesty. Gil had a patented response for those comparisons to Lou Gehrig. "Gehrig had one advantage over me," he'd say. "He was a better ballplayer." This down-to-earth attitude endeared Hodges to Dodgers fans everywhere.

"Gil had powerful muscles and a gentle voice," wrote *New York Times* columnist Joe Durso. "He helped old ladies across the street and young players across the infield. He was reverent, friendly, strong, and silent. He had a reputation for shooting straight and he even kept his hands in his back pockets when he argued with umpires. He was, kind of, a middle-aged Eagle Scout."

Gil was born on April 4, 1924, in the small town of Princeton, Indiana. His father, Charles, was a coal miner who lost several toes and his right eye in a mining accident.

Gil's family moved to Petersburg, Indiana, when he was a boy, and he quickly became involved in sports. Gil excelled on his high school teams, winning varsity letters in track, basketball, and, of course, baseball. He played American Legion baseball for two summers and was offered a minor-league contract by the Tigers. But Gil's love of baseball was mainly for the strategy. He decided to follow his brother to St. Joseph's College in Indiana and take up a coaching career.

Coaching did not pan out, and Gil went to work as a drill press operator in a local machine shop. He played baseball in his spare time for the company team. The Brooklyn Dodgers organization remembered him as a high school star and they sent a scout to Indiana to watch one of his company games. The Dodgers were impressed with Gil's all-around skills and in 1943 they signed him up. At the age of nineteen, Gil became a Dodger.

Gil's major-league debut was less than inspiring. In the only game he played in 1943, late in the season, he struck out twice and walked. When the season ended, Gil, like many other young men, wanted to serve his country in World War II. He joined the marines.

During World War II, the Hodges legend began to spread. Although Gil did not speak much about his adventures in the jungles of the Pacific, one of his fellow soldiers, who later became his teammate, did. "We didn't know who he was at first," recalled former Dodgers third baseman Don Hooke, "but we kept hearing about a jungle fighter that was killing [the enemy] with his bare hands."

After the war, in 1946, Hodges was assigned to the Dodgers' minor-league team in the Piedmont League. He played catcher for the Newport News and led the league in fielding average while hitting a tidy .278.

Gil was called up to catch for the Dodgers in 1947, but with the emergence of future Hall of Fame catcher Roy Campanella, he was moved to first base. It turned out to be one of the best moves that Brooklyn manager Leo Durocher ever made.

"I put a first baseman's mitt on our rookie catcher," Durocher recalled, "and told him to have some fun. Three days later I was looking at a great first baseman."

Gil established himself as a master around the first base bag.

Other players joked that he did not need a glove since his hands were so big. His fancy footwork sometimes had opposing players accusing him of not having his foot on the base while making a putout. This became known as the neighborhood play because it appeared as if his foot was not on the base but just in the "neighborhood" of it.

"He was one of the most graceful first basemen I've ever seen," said Hall of Fame player and manager Casey Stengel. "What was also remarkable about Gil was that he was a great fielding first baseman and a great fielding catcher."

In 1948 Gil established himself as the everyday first baseman and drove in 70 runs while batting .249. In 1949 he really found his hitting stroke. Gil more than doubled his home run total and started his string of seven consecutive seasons driving in 100 or more runs with 155 RBIs. He also led all first basemen with a .995 fielding average, making only seven errors and amassing 1,336 putouts. His clutch hitting helped lead a powerful Brooklyn team to the World Series. Gil connected for a home run and 4 RBIs in the Series, but the Dodgers lost to the Yankees four games to one.

That year, 1949, also marked the season that started Gil on his home run streak. For eleven straight seasons he would hit at least 22 home runs a year.

The next year, Gil established himself as a serious home run threat, hitting 32 homers and driving in 113 runs. And on August 31, 1950, he gave baseball a thrill by belting four home runs in a game.

Gil hit four homers and a single that day, leading the home-town Dodgers to a 19–3 trouncing of the Boston Braves. His first dinger was a two-run shot that came in the second inning against future Hall of Fame pitcher Warren Spahn. The next inning he smashed a three-run homer against Normie Roy, and then he grounded out to third in the fourth inning. He hit a two-run home run against Bob Hall in the sixth inning, singled sharply to the left in the seventh, and swatted a final two-run homer against future all-star pitcher Johnny Antonelli in the eighth.

"There were only 14,226 cash customers present to see Hodges' almost unprecedented feat—certainly unprecedented for a Dodger—but they enjoyed every minute of it," reported the *New York Times*.

The Dodgers returned to the World Series in 1952, only to lose to the Yankees once again, this time in seven games. That Series proved especially frustrating for Gil. He set a World Series record by going hitless in all 21 of his at bats. He also made an error.

His horrendous hitting slump carried into the early part of 1953, when his batting average was below .200 for the first six weeks of the season. Gil received hundreds of letters from adoring fans encouraging him and offering batting tips. In what has become a well-known baseball story, a Brooklyn priest stood up in front of his congregation and told them to keep the commandments and say a prayer for Gil Hodges.

"Brooklyn fans are the greatest," Hodges said during his slump. "They are very patient with me."

After his brutal World Series performance, Gil made appearances around Brooklyn, heating his bats up over fires to make them hot for the upcoming season. Whether or not it was divine intervention, heating up his bats, or just a solid ballplayer reaching down and pulling himself out of the slump,

Gil's bats began to belt baseballs by the end of May. Gil rebounded to make 1953 one of his finest seasons. He batted .302, smacked 31 home runs, and drove in 122 runs. He led the Dodgers to their second consecutive World Series appearance, and although Brooklyn lost to the crosstown Yankees again, Gil had a great series, hitting .364, with a home run.

Brooklyn finally did beat the Yankees in 1955, during a seven-game World Series that Gil seemed to win all by himself. He batted .292, with a home run and 5 runs batted in. His home run in game four gave Brooklyn the lead in the Series, and he drove in the only two runs of the seventh and deciding game.

Two years later, Dodgers owner Walter O'Malley broke the hearts of Brooklyn's fans when he announced the club was moving to Los Angeles. Although the Dodgers were making money in Brooklyn, O'Malley had the foresight to tap into a new market that was starving for baseball. A shrewd business-man, O'Malley also arranged for the New York Giants to move to San Francisco. In one deal he had moved the National League's oldest rivalry from one coast to the other, leaving New York without a National League team.

Although Gil played for the Los Angeles Dodgers, he and his family still lived in Brooklyn. He was known in his neighbor-hood as the Pride of Flatbush.

New York received another National League team in 1962 when the expansion Mets were born. Chosen in the expansion draft, Gil finished his playing career with the Mets. Hodges remained a fan favorite, although at age thirty-eight his hitting skills were clearly diminishing. In 1963 Gil was traded to the Washington Senators. He never played a game for the Senators, but he fulfilled his lifelong dream when he took over as their manager on May 22, 1963.

He managed the Senators, who later became the Texas Rangers, until 1967, when he returned to the Mets as their manager. This was a true challenge. The Mets were a pitiful team who had the reputation of being the clowns of baseball. Gil wanted them to take themselves seriously. His arrival changed their image, although the lowly Mets finished in ninth place in 1968.

In 1969, he led the "Miracle Mets" to an improbable World Series triumph over the powerful Baltimore Orioles. It was a truly amazing feat. Hodges took a last-place team that only seven years earlier had lost a record 120 games and guided them to the World Championship.

Although many credited Gil's crafty managing and shrewd platooning as the main reasons for the Mets' rise, he preferred to praise his players. "It was a colossal thing that they did," he said immediately after the Mets disposed of the Orioles in just five games. "These young men showed that you can realize the most impossible dream of all."

In honor of the man who managed the worst team in baseball to their first World Championship, the New York Mets retired Gil's number, 14. Although Gil was one of the most respected sluggers of his time, people will ultimately remember him for his first love, managing, and for the unbelievable championship that he brought to New York baseball fans.

Hodges, Gilbert Raymond

Born Gilbert Ray Hodges.
b. Apr. 4, 1924, Princeton, Ind. d. Apr. 2, 1972, West Palm Beach, Fla.
Manager 1963–1971.

YEAR TEAM	GAMES	BA	SA	AB	H	2B	3B
1946 BKN N	1	.000	.000	2	0	0	0
1947	28	.156	.260	77	12	3	1
1948	134	.249	.376	481	120	18	5
1949	156	.285	.453	596	170	23	4
1950	153	.283	.508	561	159	26	2
1951	158	.268	.527	582	156	25	3
1952	153	.254	.500	508	129	27	1
1953	141	.302	.550	520	157	22	7
1954	154	.304	.579	579	176	23	5
1955	150	.289	.500	546	158	24	5
1956	153	.265	.507	550	146	29	4
1957	150	.299	.511	579	173	28	7
1958 LA N	141	.259	.434	475	123	15	1
1959	124	.276	.513	413	114	19	2
1960	101	.198	.371	197	39	8	1
1961	109	.242	.372	215	52	4	0
1962 NY N	54	.252	.427	127	32	1	0
1963	11	.227	.227	22	5	0	0
18 yrs.	2071	.273	.487	7030	1921	295	48

WORLD SERIES

YEAR TEAM	GAMES	BA	SA	AB	H	2B	3B
1947 BKN N	1	.000	.000	1	0	0	0
1949	5	.235	.412	17	4	0	0
1952	7	.000	.000	21	0	0	0
1953	6	.364	.500	22	8	0	0
1955	7	.292	.417	24	7	0	0
1956	7	.304	.522	23	7	2	0
1959 LA N	6	.391	.609	23	9	0	1
7 yrs.	39	.267	.412	131	35	2	1

YEAR	HR	HR%	R	RBI	BB	SO	SB
1946	0	0.0	0	0	1	2	1
1947	1	1.3	9	7	14	19	0
1948	11	2.3	48	70	43	61	7
1949	23	3.9	94	115	66	64	10
1950	32	5.7	98	113	73	73	6
1951	40	6.9	118	103	93	99	9
1952	32	6.3	87	102	107	90	2
1953	31	6.0	101	122	75	84	1
1954	42	7.3	106	130	74	84	3
1955	27	4.9	75	102	80	91	2
1956	32	5.8	86	87	76	91	3
1957	27	4.7	94	98	63	91	5
1958	22	4.6	68	64	52	87	8
1959	25	6.1	57	80	58	92	3
1960	8	4.1	22	30	26	37	0
1961	8	3.7	25	31	24	43	3
1962	9	7.1	15	17	15	27	0
1963	0	0.0	2	3	3	2	0
18 yrs.	370	5.3	1105	1274	943	1137	63

WORLD SERIES

YEAR	HR	HR%	R	RBI	BB	SO	SB
1947	0	0.0	0	0	0	1	0
1949	1	5.9	2	4	1	4	0
1952	0	0.0	1	1	5	6	0
1953	1	4.5	3	1	3	3	1
1955	1	4.2	2	5	3	2	0
1956	1	4.3	5	8	4	4	0
1959	1	4.3	2	2	1	2	0
7 yrs.	5	3.8	15	21	17	22	1

CHAPTER SIX

Joe Adcock

When Joe Adcock managed the Cleveland Indians for the 1967 season, he was severely criticized for platooning Cleveland's two best home-run hitters. Adcock had Leon Wagner and Rocky Colavito share outfield duties instead of finding room for both sluggers in the lineup. The '67 Cleveland Indians team was also hurt by injuries. They finished in eighth place, seventeen games behind first-place Boston. Adcock was fired after the season. In a way you could say that Joe Adcock's entire major-league career was hurt by injuries and platooning.

Joe Adcock belted 336 home runs during a seventeen-year career that saw him play for the Reds, Braves, Indians, and Angels. Although he played with such home-run greats as Mickey Mantle, Duke Snider, Willie Mays, and Hank Aaron,

Adcock was still considered one of the most feared home-run hitters of his time. Joe was often either platooned or on the disabled list, and he finished his career averaging only 115 games a year. Despite playing a limited schedule most seasons, Joe retired as the seventh most prolific right-handed home-run hitter. Adcock's was a career that seesawed between impressive home run statistics and the frustration of sitting on the bench because of injuries and platooning.

Joseph Wilbur Adcock was born on October 30, 1927, in the small rural town of Coushatta, Louisiana. Although he dabbled in sports throughout his childhood, Joe began to play baseball seriously when he entered Louisiana State University in 1944. Joe was a star at LSU for three years, but the lure of professional baseball proved too great. He left college in 1947 when the Cincinnati Reds signed him to a minor-league contract.

His first stop on the way to the major leagues was playing first base for Columbia, South Carolina, of the South Atlantic League. The hard-hitting right-hander collected impressive home run numbers first for Columbia and then for Tulsa of the Texas League before being called up to the majors.

When Joe reported to the Reds in 1950, Cincinnati already had a left-handed hitter, Ted Kluszewski, at first base, so a natural platoon was formed. Adcock started against lefties and Kluszewski against righties.

The platoon only lasted a short while, until Adcock volunteered to play left field in order to get both potent bats into the starting lineup. Adcock enjoyed a successful rookie campaign, playing the final seventy-five games in the outfield.

During the next two seasons, Joe was subject to more platooning and shifting between the outfield and first base. His offensive numbers suffered considerably. Most power hitters need to be in the lineup every day to find a groove. In both 1950 and 1951, Joe played only partial seasons and had fewer than 400 at bats each year. The Cincinnati Reds were disappointed with his production, and in 1953 they traded Joe to the Milwaukee Braves.

Joe was returned to first base and played a career-high 157 games for Milwaukee. He batted a respectable .285 but impressed fans the most with his extra–base hit power, collecting 33 doubles, 6 triples, 18 homers, and 80 runs batted in.

In 1954, Hank Aaron joined the club and helped form a lineup that would instill fear in National League pitchers. It was a team that would be a contender for a decade, winning two pennants and one World Series.

"We had a great lineup back then," recalled Adcock. "We had Aaron and [Eddie] Mathews, who both went into the Hall of Fame, and we had Del Crandall. Del couldn't hit like [Brooklyn's Roy] Campanella but he was definitely the best all-around catcher of his time."

In 1954, Joe batted a career-high .308 and discovered how much he loved hitting against the Brooklyn Dodgers. Joe tied a major-league record by hitting nine home runs on the road against the Dodgers that year, including four in one game.

Joe's magical weekend against Brooklyn started on July 30, 1954, when he hit a home run, a double, and a single, leading the Braves to victory. The very next day, July 31, Joe smashed four home runs and a double in a 15–7 rout of the Dodgers at Ebbets Field.

Joe's home runs were hit against four different Dodgers pitchers. He connected for a solo homer against Dodgers starter Don Newcombe in the second inning. Erv Palica came on to relieve Newcombe, but the Braves batted around, and Joe slammed a double his second time up in that inning. He went on to smash a three-run home run against Palica in the fifth, a two-run shot in the seventh against Pete Wojey, and his fourth of the day, a solo homer in the ninth, against Johnny Podres. Joe's eighteen total bases in one game still stand as a major-league record.

"What an unbelievable thrill," a laughing Adcock told reporters after the game. "I was using a borrowed bat all the time. I broke my regular bat last night, so today I used one belonging to [reserve catcher] Charley White. Boy, I could hardly lift it. It's the heaviest on the team."

Adcock laughed again when asked to explain his unusual success against the Brooklyn Dodgers. "I don't know what it is but I think I would hit 35 homers a year if I played here all the time."

Joe was hailed as a hero back in Milwaukee. Full-color photographs of him graced the front page of the *Milwaukee Journal,* and a black-and-white photo appeared on page one of the *Milwaukee Sentinel.* It was very uncommon in those days to have a sports personality on the front page of the newspaper.

Joe's batting stayed hot throughout the weekend. The next day, August 1, he cracked a double his first time up. The Dodgers pitchers finally retaliated against his onslaught during his second at bat, when he was hit by Clem Labine's pitched ball.

In 1955, Joe missed most of the season with a broken arm but still managed to hack 15 home runs in only 288 at bats. He rebounded in 1956 to have his best offensive season ever. Joe continued his uncanny assault on Brooklyn Dodgers pitching that year when he blasted a National League–record 13 round-trippers against the Dodgers.

Apparently destined for more greatness and poised to help the Braves to a pennant, Joe endured his most frustrating season in 1957. He broke his leg while sliding early in the year and was forced to sit and watch as the Braves captured first place and headed toward the pennant without him. He returned to the plate in late June, just in time to hit 12 home runs in 209 at bats, and to face the New York Yankees in the World Series.

Joe only batted .200 in the Series, but drove in two big runs to help the Braves capture the World Championship in seven games over the Yanks.

Joe considered winning the World Series the biggest thrill he ever had—even more satisfying than his four home-run game.

In 1958, Joe was back to platooning with other players and shifting back and forth from the outfield to first base. Although he had only 320 at bats that season, he did well at the plate. The Braves made it back to the World Series in 1958, and Joe batted .308 with four singles, but the Yankees swept the Braves in four games.

From 1959 through 1961, Joe enjoyed three very productive seasons, in spite of limited playing time. The home-run totals began to mount, and it makes one wonder just how many home runs Joe would have hit had he been able to collect 500 at bats a season. His powerful home-run stroke and equally impressive totals suggest that he might have been one of the game's elite home-run champions. In 1961, Joe finally increased his playing time, appearing in 152 games and belting 35 home runs, with a career-high 108 RBIs.

Joe's production slipped considerably in 1962. Although he hit 29 homers, his batting average and RBI totals were disappointing. He was traded to the Cleveland Indians in 1963 and then to the Los Angeles Angels in 1964, where he finished his playing career. Even as he aged, Joe maintained that powerful stroke, filled with promises of more home runs. His best season after his Milwaukee Braves days was 1964, when he smashed 21 home runs for the Angels.

Joe retired after the 1966 baseball season with a career total of 336 home runs.

He managed the Cleveland Indians to an eighth-place finish in 1967 and was fired after one season. He went on to manage Seattle of the Pacific Coast League in 1968 before retiring from baseball for good.

It is amazing that someone who spent most of his career as a platoon ballplayer amassed such staggering totals. He collected 1,122 RBIs, 295 doubles, and 35 triples and played in two World Series and the 1960 all-star game. Not bad for a part-time player.

Adcock, Joseph Wilbur
b. Oct. 30, 1927, Coushatta, La.
Manager 1967.

YEAR	TEAM	GAMES	BA	SA	AB	H	2B	3B
1950	CIN N	102	.293	.406	372	109	16	1
1951		113	.243	.380	395	96	16	4
1952		117	.278	.460	378	105	22	4
1953	MIL N	157	.285	.453	590	168	33	6
1954		133	.308	.520	500	154	27	5
1955		84	.264	.469	288	76	14	0
1956		137	.291	.597	454	132	23	1
1957		65	.287	.541	209	60	13	2
1958		105	.275	.506	320	88	15	1
1959		115	.292	.535	404	118	19	2
1960		138	.298	.500	514	153	21	4
1961		152	.285	.507	562	160	20	0
1962		121	.248	.506	391	97	12	1
1963	CLE A	97	.251	.420	283	71	7	1
1964	LA A	118	.268	.475	366	98	13	0
1965	CAL A	122	.241	.401	349	84	14	0
1966		83	.273	.576	231	63	10	3
17 yrs.		1959	.277	.485	6606	1832	295	35

WORLD SERIES

YEAR	TEAM	GAMES	BA	SA	AB	H	2B	3B
1957	MIL N	5	.200	.200	15	3	0	0
1958		4	.308	.308	13	4	0	0
2 yrs.		9	.250	.250	28	7	0	0

YEAR	HR	HR%	R	RBI	BB	SO	SB
1950	8	2.2	46	55	24	24	2
1951	10	2.5	40	47	24	29	1
1952	13	3.4	43	52	23	38	1
1953	18	3.1	71	80	42	82	3
1954	23	4.6	73	87	44	58	1
1955	15	5.2	40	45	31	44	0
1956	38	8.4	76	103	32	86	1
1957	12	5.7	31	38	20	51	0
1958	19	5.9	40	54	21	63	0
1959	25	6.2	53	76	32	77	0
1960	25	4.9	55	91	46	86	2
1961	35	6.2	77	108	59	94	2
1962	29	7.4	48	78	50	91	2
1963	13	4.6	28	49	30	53	1
1964	21	5.7	39	64	48	61	0
1965	14	4.0	30	47	37	74	2
1966	18	7.8	33	48	31	48	2
17 yrs.	336	5.1	823	1122	594	1059	20

WORLD SERIES

YEAR	HR	HR%	R	RBI	BB	SO	SB
1957	0	0.0	1	2	0	2	0
1958	0	0.0	1	0	1	3	0
2 yrs.	0	0.0	2	2	1	5	0

CHAPTER SEVEN

Rocky Colavito

D on't knock the Rock!"
That was the call that echoed throughout Cleveland whenever popular Indians slugger Rocky Colavito was in a hitting slump.

The boyishly handsome Colavito captured the hearts of Cleveland fans with his good looks, his charisma, and, most of all, his knack for hitting monstrous home runs. He was so popular among Indians fans that in 1976, eight years after retiring from baseball as a player, he was voted the most memorable personality in the team's history.

Rocky was born Rocco Domenico Colavito on August 10, 1933, to Angelina and Rocco Colavito, Sr., in the Bronx, New York. Rocky was the youngest of five children. He attended Public School No. 4 and Theodore Roosevelt High School, where he fell in love with the game of baseball. In 1949, at the age of sixteen, Rocky began playing semiprofessional ball. Rocky had a rifle for an arm and was an excellent pitcher as well as an excellent all-around outfielder. Having attracted scouts from all over the big leagues, Rocky signed with the Cleveland Indians as a pitcher-outfielder in 1951 and began the long climb to the major leagues.

In 1951 Rocky played with Daytona Beach of the Florida State League and slugged 23 home runs with 111 RBIs. Although he was blessed with a strong throwing arm, it was clear that Rocky's strength was his hitting. He soon gave up pitching and began playing the outfield on a full-time basis.

The next year, Rocky was promoted twice. He split the 1952 season between Cedar Rapids, Iowa, and Spartanburg, South Carolina. In 1953, he led the Class A Eastern League with 28 home runs and 121 RBIs while playing for Reading, Pennsylvania. The next season, in Indianapolis, Indiana, Rocky dominated the American Association with 38 home runs and 116 runs batted in. He remained in Indianapolis until the fall of 1955. Because major-league teams are allowed to call up extra players for the pennant drive, Rocky got his first taste of the big leagues that September, appearing in five games for the Indians. He began the 1956 season at San Diego of the Pacific Coast League, and in July the Indians summoned the hard-hitting Rocky to Cleveland.

The six-foot–three-inch Colavito made an immediate impression. He slugged 21 home runs in just more than half a season. That started a string of eleven consecutive seasons with twenty or more home runs. In 1957, Colavito was plagued a bit by the sophomore jinx. His batting average suffered and he was prone to lapses in the field. Eager to show off his strong throwing arm, Rocky often missed the cutoff man and overthrew bases. He committed a career-high 11 errors that season.

Rocky worked with Cleveland manager Joe Gordon on his swing and his fielding and soon he made himself a complete player. He learned to think more in the field and used his rifle arm to become an excellent right fielder. He was soon to be compared with future Hall of Famer Roberto Clemente, the hard-throwing right fielder for the Pittsburgh Pirates. Manager Gordon's greatest accomplishment, however, was getting Rocky to cut down on his swings. This helped raise his batting average and reduce his strikeouts.

By this time Rocky had a huge following in Cleveland. These fans were behind him every step of the way. "He was definitely a fan favorite," recalled New York sportswriter Jim O'Toole. "And why not? He was a good looking guy, always smiling, waved to the stands, had a great arm and most of all he was a longball man. The fans love a longball man."

In 1958, Colavito terrorized American League pitching with a .303 batting average, 41 round-trippers, and 113 runs batted in. In 1959 he became the first Cleveland Indian ever to have two 40-homer seasons when he belted 42 homers, tying Minnesota slugger and future Hall of Famer Harmon Killebrew for the league lead.

Sportswriters and fans alike were already comparing the twenty-five-year-old Rocky with Babe Ruth. The *Sporting News* said that Rocky was the "most likely player to emulate—and possibly surpass—Babe Ruth's record of 60 home runs in one season."

On June 10, 1959, one week after the *Sporting News* article was written, Rocky fueled everyone's imagination when he smashed four consecutive home runs in a single game. "That was a fine compliment the *Sporting News* paid me. Maybe this will make the story look a little better," Rocky said.

Rocky's four home runs led the visiting Indians to an 11–8 slug-fest victory against the Baltimore Orioles. Rocky walked his first time up in the first inning. Then, in the third inning, he connected for a two-run homer against Jerry Walker. He hit a solo home run in the fifth against reliever Arnie Portocarrero. Rocky victimized Portocarrero again in the sixth for a two-run shot before belting a solo shot in the ninth against relief pitcher Ernie Johnson.

"Those who are familiar with the Baltimore ball park are prepared to argue that Rocky's accomplishment had to be greater than all the others [who have hit four home runs in a game]. It's the most difficult home-run park in the majors. No team, much less an individual, had hit more than three home runs a night there until Rocky came along," wrote the *Sporting News* columnist Hal Lebovitz.

After hitting his fourth home run, Rocky leaped into the swarm of teammates who were waiting for him at home plate. He jumped up and down, yelling "Yahoo" and "Yipee," before shaking the hands of everyone in sight.

"The players were more subdued," recalled manager Gordon. "They seemed stunned to believe they had actually witnessed the feat."

When Rocky was told that the only other player to hit four home runs in four consecutive at bats was Yankees legend Lou Gehrig, he sighed. "Gehrig was my favorite when I was a small boy," Rocky said. "My brother Vito played first base and Gehrig was his hero. So he became my hero, too."

The fans back in Cleveland showed their appreciation simply by buying tickets for future ball games. Credited to Colavito's batting and the fine overall play of the Indians ball club, the 1957 attendance figures almost doubled. The team's first Sunday home game after Rocky's great day brought in an astounding 21,000 fans who bought tickets at the gate.

The next spring, Cleveland Indians fans had their hearts broken when Rocky was traded to the Detroit Tigers for American League batting champ Harvey Kuenn, who had batted .353 the year before. Some speculated that Cleveland general manager Frank Lane based the trade on pure economics. He was not happy that Rocky had hit 42 home runs. In fact, he had put a clause in Rocky's contract that rewarded Rocky for hitting fewer than 40 home runs a season. The Indians management did not want to have to pay out what the game's top sluggers were getting, and although Kuenn was a good hitter, he rarely hit more than 9 home runs a season.

The story made headlines all over Cleveland, and the Indians organization was besieged by phone calls complaining of the trade. "The phones started ringing almost immediately. Lane was castigated by everyone. Calls came in from all over and Lane was called every conceivable name in the book," wrote Detroit sportswriter Joe Falls.

Lane antagonized Rocky's fans further by saying, "What's the problem? All I did was trade a hamburger for a steak."

Coincidentally, Rocky's new team, the Detroit Tigers, opened the 1960 season in Cleveland. This gave his fans in

Cleveland a chance to say good-bye. There were banners and signs all over Municipal Stadium to greet him. WE LOVE YOU, ROCKY, YOU'LL ALWAYS BE OURS, and FOREVER AND EVER, ROCKY were some that were draped over the right-field fence.

The game lasted fourteen innings. Rocky struck out four times, hit into a double play, and popped out. Actually, Rocky struggled with his stroke for the entire season. It seemed as if he could not adjust to playing in Detroit. He also had to endure an entirely new situation: Rocco Colavito was booed by Tigers fans when he did not perform well. He knocked in only 87 runs and did not enjoy the immense popularity of his Cleveland days. Rocky's replacement, Kuenn, was initially booed in Cleveland, but he slowly won the fans over by batting .308.

The next year, 1961, Rocky was more determined than ever. He put together a great season, hitting .290, smashing 45 home runs, and knocking in 140 runs.

Rocky lasted four years in Detroit and collected some pretty impressive numbers. He hit 139 homers and drove in 430 runs for the Tigers. He was traded to the Kansas City Athletics in 1964 and slugged 34 homers and 102 RBIs. The Indians, on a downhill slide and struggling to win back fan support, brought Rocky back to Cleveland in 1965. He responded with 26 homers and led the American League in runs batted in and walks. He also set an American League record for outfielders by playing in 234 consecutive errorless games, from September 6, 1964, to June 15, 1966.

In 1966, he belted 30 home runs, but his overall offensive production dropped dramatically. In 1967, he was being platooned in right field with Leon Wagner. Rocky was not happy with the situation and accused Cleveland general manager

Gabe Paul of forcing manager Joe Adcock to platoon him. He hinted that he wanted to be traded but did not demand it. Paul traded him to the Chicago White Sox anyway. Colavito finished his playing career in 1968 with the Los Angeles Dodgers and the New York Yankees.

Rocky made the *Sporting News* all-star team in 1961 and played in eight all-star games, from 1959 to 1966. Rocky is also the last nonpitcher to record a pitching victory. He picked up the win pitching in relief for the Yankees in 1968.

Rocky scouted part-time for the Yankees in 1969 and again in 1973. He returned to Cleveland as a coach from 1976 until 1978. He coached the Kansas City Royals in 1982 and 1983 before retiring from baseball for good.

Although the Rock is gone from baseball, his powerful home run swing, his cannon of an arm, his boyish good looks, and the special relationship he enjoyed with his dedicated fans are legendary.

Colavito, Rocco Domenico
b. Aug. 10, 1933, Bronx, N.Y.

YEAR	TEAM	GAMES	BA	SA	AB	H	2B	3B
1955	CLE A	5	.444	.667	9	4	2	0
1956		101	.286	.531	322	89	11	4
1957		134	.252	.471	461	116	26	0
1958		143	.303	.620	489	148	26	3
1959		154	.257	.512	588	151	24	0
1960	DET A	145	.249	.474	555	138	18	1
1961		163	.290	.580	583	169	30	2
1962		161	.273	.514	601	164	30	2
1963		160	.271	.437	597	162	29	2
1964	KC A	160	.274	.507	588	161	31	2
1965	CLE A	162	.387	.468	592	170	25	2
1966		151	.238	.432	533	127	13	0
1967	2 teams CLE A (63G—.241) CHI A (60G—.221)							
"	total	123	.231	.333	381	88	13	1
1968	2 teams LA A (40G—.204) NY A (39G—.220)							
"	total	79	.211	.373	204	43	5	2
14 yrs.		1841	.266	.489	6503	1730	283	21

YEAR	HR	HR%	R	RBI	BB	SO	SB
1955	0	0.0	3	0	0	2	0
1956	21	6.5	55	65	49	46	0
1957	25	5.4	66	84	71	80	1
1958	41	8.4	80	113	84	89	0
1959	42	7.1	90	111	71	86	3
1960	35	6.3	67	87	53	80	3
1961	45	7.7	129	140	113	75	1
1962	37	6.2	90	112	96	68	2
1963	22	3.7	91	91	84	78	0
1964	34	5.8	89	102	83	56	3
1965	26	4.4	92	108	93	63	1
1966	30	5.6	68	72	76	81	2
1967 " total	8	2.1	30	50	49	41	3
1968 " total	8	3.9	21	24	29	35	0
14 yrs.	374	5.8	9718	1159	951	880	19

CHAPTER EIGHT

Willie Mays

Willie Mays summed up his baseball career as honestly as he could. "I think I was the best ballplayer I ever saw," he said after being told of his election to the Baseball Hall of Fame. "There wasn't anything I couldn't do."

He was right.

Willie Mays did it all. He hit for power and average. He stole bases and tore up the base paths with reckless abandon. He was a remarkable center fielder who holds the record for amassing 7,095 putouts during his glorious twenty-two-year career with the Giants and Mets.

Willie was named after his father, William Howard Mays, Sr., when he was born on May 6, 1931, in Westfield, Alabama.

Willie's father played baseball with his son every chance he could and instilled in Willie a desire to excel. In addition to working in a steel mill, William Sr. played professional baseball with the Birmingham Black Barons of the Negro Leagues.

Blacks were not permitted to play in the major leagues until Jackie Robinson broke the color barrier and signed with the Brooklyn Dodgers in 1947. Before then, black ballplayers could only play in the Negro Leagues.

The Negro Leagues were formed in 1920 and actually existed until 1960. The accomplishments of the Negro League ballplayers did not go unnoticed. Quite a few of them, such as James "Cool Papa" Bell and Ray Dandridge were inducted into the Baseball Hall of Fame without ever having played in a major-league game.

Willie Mays, Jr., was a tremendous athlete who was a star in baseball, basketball, and football during his years at Fairfax Industrial High School in Birmingham, Alabama. But baseball was his love. After all, it was in his blood.

By the time Willie was sixteen years old, he had baseball scouts following his every move on the field. Willie's talent was so natural that playing professional ball seemed just a matter of time. Willie joined up with the Black Barons in 1947, when he was seventeen, and was a star with them while Robinson was a star for the Dodgers.

The New York Giants signed Willie in 1950 and assigned him to one of their minor-league teams, Trenton of the Interstate League. Willie batted .353 during his only season at Trenton, raising a lot of eyebrows. The next spring Willie was promoted to the Giants' triple-A team, the Minneapolis Millers of the American Association. Now he was just one step from the major leagues.

Willie did not last a full season in Minneapolis. By the end of May 1951, the Giants had no choice but to call him up to the big leagues. After all, the young outfielder was the owner of a .477 batting average (an astonishing 71 hits in 149 at bats).

"Baseball was always an easy game for me," Willie said during his Hall of Fame press conference. "It always came natural."

That was not entirely true. Willie experienced some anxious moments during his first week of facing major-league pitching. He remained hitless during his first twelve at bats and actually looked overwhelmed at times.

"Send me back to Minneapolis," he told Giants manager Leo Durocher. "I'm not ready to play here." Durocher gave him a pep talk and insisted that Willie was his center fielder for good.

The next night Willie collected his first major-league hit. It was a home run against future Hall of Famer Warren Spahn, and from then on there was no looking back. Willie had found his groove. He became the spark during the Giants' classic 1951 pennant race with the Brooklyn Dodgers, which ended with Bobby Thomson's "shot heard 'round the world." The powerful Mays was on deck when Thomson connected. Although the Giants eventually lost the World Series to their crosstown rivals, the New York Yankees, Willie was voted baseball's Rookie of the Year. He had batted .274 with 20 home runs and 68 runs batted in.

Willie's career was put on hold when he was drafted into the U.S. Army. He missed most of the 1952 season and all of 1953. Imagine the numbers Willie would have posted if he had not been drafted: He missed almost two full seasons of his career and still blasted 660 home runs (third to Hank Aaron's 756 and Babe Ruth's 714), drove in 1,903 runs, batted a lifetime .302, and stole over 300 bases.

After completing his army service, Willie returned for the 1954 season without missing a beat. His batting average, extra-base hits, and RBI totals led the Giants to another National League pennant. Mays was voted the league's Most Valuable Player that year.

It was during this time that Willie was dubbed the Say Hey Kid by New York sportswriter Barney Kremenko. Willie used to yell "Say hey" as a form of saying hello. Kremenko heard him, wrote about it in his column, and the nickname stuck.

While Willie was dominating with his bat, he was also dominating with his glove. He patrolled one of baseball's deepest center fields at New York's Polo Grounds. "It doesn't matter where you hit the ball," said Brooklyn slugger Gil Hodges. "Wherever you hit, Willie Mays is right there."

During the 1954 World Series, Willie made one of the greatest catches of all time. The score was tied late in the first game when Cleveland Indians slugger Vic Wertz came to bat with two runners on base. Wertz launched a rocket to the deepest part of center field at the Polo Grounds. The ball was well over Willie's head, so he turned his back completely to home plate and raced for the center field wall. As he neared the 430-foot sign, Willie caught the ball over his right shoulder. He immediately whirled and pegged the ball back to the infield, holding the runners and squashing Cleveland's potential rally.

Over the years, Willie's style won him fans wherever he went. He often played stickball with the children in the Harlem streets near the Polo Grounds. He patented the basket catch, a one-handed grab with the glove held at the waist, facing up, which made even the hardest play seem ordinary. He was the winner of the Gold Glove award for twelve consecutive seasons, from 1957 to 1968. He ran the bases hard every time, and he slid even harder. He might have collected more than his 338 career stolen bases if the Giants had not asked him to stop stealing. Willie was too valuable to the team to risk being injured while stealing a base. And, of course, he was always potent with the bat. But it was the way he played the game that made the fans sit up and take notice.

"Too many guys look at the statistics and nothing else," wrote the late New York sportswriter Dick Young. "Stats don't tell the story of Willie Mays. You had to see him play. You had to see that cap fly off his head as he caught a fly ball that couldn't be caught, as he took the bases, *beep-beep,* like a roadrunner, as he gunned down a man at the plate with that bazooka he used for an arm."

Willie's 1957 season marked one of the greatest batting years any ballplayer has ever had. Willie batted .333 and totaled 20 or more in the categories of doubles, triples, homers, and stolen bases.

But by 1957, the New York Giants were in financial trouble and decided to try their luck on the West Coast. The Giants moved to San Francisco in time for the 1958 season.

"I've played in New York since I've been in the majors," Willie said at the time. "I love the people there. My heart will always be in New York."

The change of scenery may have bothered him emotionally, but at the plate, he was the same old Willie. He batted .347 with 29 homers.

On April 30, 1961, Willie became the seventh player since 1900 to belt four homers in one game. Willie led a 14–4 rout of the home-team Milwaukee Braves with a 420-foot solo homer off of Lew Burdette in the first, a two-run shot off of Burdette in the third, a three-run 450-foot home run in the sixth off of reliever Seth Morehead, and a two-run blast in the eighth inning against Don McMahon.

"I don't know what happened to me," a smiling Willie said after the game. "Today is easily the greatest day I've ever had. When you hit two homers in a game, that's something. You don't expect any more."

It must have been some game to watch. Hank Aaron, baseball's all-time home-run king, hit a pair for the Braves. In addition to Willie's four, the Giants hit four more. Jose Pagan hit two, and Orlando Cepeda and Felipe Alou also collected a round-tripper apiece.

"I hit three of them off of sliders and one was a sinker. But I hit them all pretty good," he said.

The winning pitcher for the Giants was Billy Loes. Loes may have been a lucky charm. He is the only player to have been present during four of the nine four home-run games in the modern era. Loes was with the Dodgers when Gil Hodges hit his four homers, was still with Brooklyn when Milwaukee's Joe Adcock hit his against the Dodgers, and was with Baltimore when Cleveland's Rocky Colavito hit his.

Willie Mays continued to pound baseballs and smash home runs for twelve more seasons. Along the way, he was awarded another Most Valuable Player award in 1965 and was named Player of the Decade for the 1960s by the *Sporting News.*

Willie was able to finish his glorious career back in New York when the Giants traded him to the Mets in 1972. In his first game for the Mets, May 13, 1972, Willie smacked a home run against the Giants.

Willie retired in 1973 after helping the Mets win the National League pennant. He was elected to the Hall of Fame in 1979.

These days, when Willie is not playing golf, he stays involved in baseball by serving as the special assistant to the president and general manager of the San Francisco Giants. He also spends time broadcasting Giants games on cable television.

"I played mainly for the enjoyment of the people who came out to see me play every day," Willie says. "I was like the guy on a stage trying to give a good performance day in and day out. To me, that's more important than having one great day and a bunch of average ones."

Mays, William Howard, Jr. (Say Hey)

b. May 6, 1931, Westfield, Ala.
Hall of Fame 1979.

YEAR	TEAM	GAMES	BA	SA	AB	H	2B	3B
1951	NY N	121	.274	.472	464	127	22	5
1952		34	.236	.409	127	30	2	4
1954		151	.345	.667	565	195	33	13
1955		152	.319	.659	580	185	18	13
1956		152	.296	.557	578	171	27	8
1957		152	.333	.626	585	195	26	20
1958	SF N	152	.347	.583	600	208	33	11
1959		151	.313	.583	575	180	43	5
1960		153	.319	.555	595	190	29	12
1961		154	.308	.584	572	176	32	3
1962		162	.304	.615	621	189	36	5
1963		157	.314	.582	596	187	32	7
1964		157	.296	.607	578	171	21	9
1965		157	.317	.645	558	177	21	3
1966		152	.288	.556	552	159	29	4
1967		141	.263	.453	486	128	22	2
1968		148	.289	.488	498	144	20	5
1969		117	.283	.437	403	114	17	3
1970		139	.291	.506	478	139	15	2
1971		136	.271	.482	417	113	24	5
1972	2 teams SF N (19G—.184) NY N (69G—.267)							
"	total	88	.250	.402	244	61	11	1
1973	NY N	66	.211	.344	209	44	10	0
22 yrs.		2992	.302	.557	10881	3283	523	140
		6th		10th	6th	9th		

LEAGUE CHAMPIONSHIP SERIES

1971	SF N	4	.267	.600	15	4	2	0
1973	NY N	1	.333	.333	3	1	0	0
2 yrs.		5	.278	.556	18	5	2	0

WORLD SERIES

1951	NY N	6	.182	.182	22	4	0	0
1954		4	.286	.357	14	4	1	0
1962	SF N	7	.250	.321	28	7	2	0
1973	NY N	3	.286	.286	7	2	0	0
4 yrs.		20	.239	.282	71	17	3	0

78

YEAR	HR	HR%	R	RBI	BB	SO	SB
1951	20	4.3	59	68	56	60	7
1952	4	3.1	17	23	16	17	4
1954	41	7.3	119	110	66	57	8
1955	51	8.8	123	127	79	60	24
1956	36	6.2	101	84	68	65	40
1957	35	6.0	112	97	76	62	38
1958	29	4.8	121	96	78	56	31
1959	34	5.9	125	104	65	58	27
1960	29	4.9	107	103	61	70	25
1961	40	7.0	129	123	81	77	18
1962	49	7.9	130	141	78	85	18
1963	38	6.4	115	103	66	83	8
1964	47	8.1	121	111	82	72	19
1965	52	9.3	118	112	76	71	9
1966	37	6.7	99	103	70	81	5
1967	22	4.5	83	70	51	92	6
1968	23	4.6	84	79	67	81	12
1969	13	3.2	64	58	49	71	6
1970	28	5.9	94	83	79	90	5
1971	18	4.3	82	61	112	123	23
1972							
" total	8	3.3	35	22	60	48	4
1973	6	2.9	24	25	27	47	1
22 yrs.	660	6.1	2062	1903	1463	1526	338
	3rd		5th	7th			

LEAGUE CHAMPIONSHIP SERIES

YEAR	HR	HR%	R	RBI	BB	SO	SB
1971	1	6.7	2	3	3	3	1
1973	0	0.0	1	1	0	0	0
2 yrs.	1	5.6	3	4	3	3	1

WORLD SERIES

YEAR	HR	HR%	R	RBI	BB	SO	SB
1951	0	0.0	1	1	2	2	0
1954	0	0.0	4	3	4	1	1
1962	0	0.0	3	1	1	5	1
1973	0	0.0	1	1	0	1	0
4 yrs.	0	0.0	9	6	7	9	2

CHAPTER NINE

Mike Schmidt

E veryone pretty much figured that Michael Jack Schmidt would hit a lot of major-league home runs. That is, if he got to stay in the major leagues. You see, Mike Schmidt had a big problem: He could not stop striking out. Who would believe that Hall of Fame prospect Mike Schmidt once had a very serious lack of confidence? Everyone believed in Mike Schmidt, but he had to believe in himself first.

In fact, Mike did not even bat .200 his first full season in the majors. He did hit 18 home runs, but he posted a paltry .196 batting average with a whopping 136 strikeouts.

Mike Schmidt was born on September 27, 1949, in Dayton, Ohio, to Jack and Louise Schmidt. Mike was exposed to sports and athletics at an early age because his parents managed a restaurant at a Dayton swimming club. The club gave Mike access to many other sports as well.

Mike played baseball for Dayton's Fairview High School. During his junior year, he began to show promising power and attracted attention from big-league scouts.

Philadelphia scout Tony Lucadello was interested. "I followed Mike through his junior year of high school. He was a switch hitter and he wasn't really ready for professional baseball when he graduated. I thought he'd be one of these ballplayers who'd be a late arrival, but I knew he was going to make it," Lucadello recalled.

In 1967, Mike won a baseball scholarship to Ohio University. Mike started out slowly on the college team, splitting time between third base, shortstop, and second base during his first three seasons. He also batted left- and right-handed. After his junior year, Mike went to play in a league with collegiate all-stars from all over the country. Mike performed well in that off-season tournament and gained the confidence he needed to excel.

In his senior year, Mike was named a College All-American. He established school records for home runs with 10, walks with 38, and runs scored with 45. "He had a fantastic senior year," Lucadello said. "I brought some people to see him play."

Lucadello convinced the Phillies to consider Schmidt's potential, and Mike was drafted in the second round of the 1971 amateur draft. "It was quite a simple signing," Lucadello said. "He was a college senior that just wanted to play ball."

Mike was assigned to Reading, Pennsylvania, where he played shortstop. He suffered through a poor season, batting only .211 with 8 home runs, 31 RBIs, 23 errors, and 66 strikeouts in seventy-four games. During the off-season Mike played in the Instructional League, where he manned third base exclusively. Much more comfortable at third, Mike put up some excellent numbers. The next season, he played second and third base for Eugene, Oregon, and had an outstanding season, batting .291 with 26 homers and 91 RBIs. By this time, Mike had finished experimenting with switch-hitting and was batting exclusively right-handed. He was still posting alarmingly high numbers of strikeouts and errors, though.

Mike was called up to the Philadelphia Phillies during September of 1972 and was platooned with regular Phillies third baseman Cesar Tovar. Mike's first full season, 1973, is one he would probably rather forget. He struck out 136 times in 132 games and managed only 72 hits in 367 at bats. Former Phillies teammate and all-star Willie Montanez nicknamed Schmidt "A-choo" for his wild swings and misses.

The Phillies were very patient and obviously saw a diamond in the rough. Philadelphia manager Danny Ozark and batting coach Bobby Wine tutored Schmidt constantly and sent him to play winter baseball in Puerto Rico to work on his swinging mechanics.

The next season, a more confident and more mechanically correct Schmidt improved dramatically. He raised his batting average by nearly 100 points and led the National League with 36 home runs. This would be the first of eight National League records for leading the league in homers. Mike also showed an excellent eye and patience at the plate; he walked 106 times.

"A guy who strikes out as much as I do had better lead the league in something," a laughing Schmidt said after winning the home run crown.

The six-foot–two-inch right-hander played much of the 1975 season with a sprained shoulder, which helps explain the 180 times he struck out. Mike managed to lead the league once again with 38 home runs, and he also stole 29 bases that year.

In 1976, Mike led the league for a third straight year with 38 home runs. He also set a modern-day National League record when, like Gehrig and Colavito, he belted four *consecutive* home runs to lead the visiting Phillies to a slug-fest victory over the Chicago Cubs.

It was April 17, 1976. With a twenty-mile-an-hour wind blowing straight out of Chicago's homer-friendly Wrigley Field, the game was bound to be a high-scoring affair. Chicago's Rick Monday had two home runs and two singles in the first four innings, helping the Cubs take a 13–2 lead. But, as they say in Chicago, when the wind is blowing out of Wrigley, no lead is safe. Ordinary fly balls become wind-blown home runs, and infield pop-ups become adventures as the ball drifts in the swirling winds. Slug fests and big come-from-behind victories are not unusual at Wrigley Field.

Schmidt had singled and grounded out against Chicago ace Rick Reuschel before his home-run barrage started. He then tagged Reuschel for a two-run homer in the fifth inning and a bases-empty shot in the seventh.

Then a Philadelphia rally was sparked, and Mike hit a three-run homer in the eighth against reliever Mike Garman.

The score was tied 15–15 when Schmidt faced Paul Reuschel, Rick's brother, in the top of the tenth. With teammate Dick Allen on first, Mike's final home run snapped the tie and gave the Phils an improbable and dramatic victory.

"I honestly wasn't trying to hit that fourth home run," a

happy Schmidt said after the game. "I was only trying to get a single to move Dick Allen into scoring position. I only wanted to win the game."

Not only did he win the game, but he added a Hollywood ending by doing it with a record-breaking fourth home run.

It turned out that Mike, who had not gotten into a good hitting groove during the first few weeks of the season, had relied on a few friends and odd superstitions to break out of his slump. Before the game, Mike borrowed an old bat from teammate Tony Taylor, and he wore Phillies infielder Terry Harmon's ratty old T-shirt beneath his uniform. Also, Philadelphia's all-star first baseman, Dick Allen, approached Mike before the game and sat him down in the dugout.

"I had a long talk with Dick Allen before the game," Mike said. "I can't really say I was down in the mouth, but he's a good friend and I needed a little boost. He gave me a solid man-to-man. He told me that we were going to mess around between innings, we're gonna have a good time today and we're gonna get back to having fun in this game."

"Don't give me any credit," Allen said after the contest was over. "I just told him to have a little fun. With all the talent he's got, he should be having fun at this game."

As usual, Mike was more concerned with how the team was doing than with his own personal statistics. "We've been off to a slow start this year," he said. "The team has been in a little slump and we had been trying to figure out what was wrong."

That same year, 1976, Mike established himself as a premier third baseman. Equipped with a powerful arm, Schmidt would patrol a deep third base on the AstroTurf at Philadelphia's Veterans Stadium. He would soon set the standard for third-base play just as Brooks Robinson did with the Baltimore Orioles during the 1960s and 1970s. Mike won the Gold Glove award for the first of eleven times in 1976.

Mike teamed up with Phillies cleanup hitter Greg "The Bull" Luzinski to form a dangerous middle to the Philadelphia batting order. Opposing pitchers were faced with pitching against the most potent home-run combination of the 1970s. From 1975 to 1980, the two sluggers combined to average 66 home runs a year and were big factors in the Phillies' three consecutive division titles, from 1976 to 1978.

The Phillies lost those three pennant bids, but finally made it to the World Series in 1980. That year, Mike belted 48 home runs with 121 runs batted in and was the runaway choice for the National League's Most Valuable Player.

The icing was added to the cake when Mike was also named the World Series Most Valuable Player after the Phillies defeated the Kansas City Royals in six games. He batted .381 and hit two home runs in the Series. He also drove in two key runs during the Phillies' final 4–1 victory for the first world championship in the team's history.

Mike was voted the league's Most Valuable Player again in 1981 during a strike-shortened season. Even then, his statistics looked as if he had played a full schedule.

Mike led the Phillies to another World Series appearance in 1983, when he belted 40 round-trippers and drove in 109 runs. This time, however, Mike suffered through a horrible World Series. The Baltimore Orioles pitchers fed him nothing but off-speed pitches. Schmidt managed only one single in twenty at bats during the five-game loss to Baltimore, and he struck out six times.

In 1986, although the Phillies finished in second place, they were more than twenty games behind the World Champion New York Mets. Mike was voted the National League's MVP for the third time. At age thirty-seven, Mike batted .290 and led the league with 119 RBIs.

Schmidt said, "Nineteen eighty-six was my most enjoyable season from a personal standpoint. From day one, I played consistently well all year. It's nice to be on a winning ball club but winning the award is nice, too."

Although 1986 was the last year that Mike would lead the league in home runs and RBIs, and was also the last time he would win a Gold Glove award, he did not slow down one step in 1987.

Mike pulverized National League pitching once again, posting impressive offensive numbers and solidifying his bid for the Hall of Fame. On April 18, Mike became only the fourteenth major-league player to hit five hundred home runs. Mike victimized Pittsburgh's Don Robinson with a two-out, ninth-inning, three-run home run, leading the Phillies to an 8–6 victory. Mike jumped up and down and pumped his fists in the air as he circled the base paths.

"You couldn't write a more perfect script," Mike said after the game. "I knew all we needed was a single to tie the score and then I saw the ball go out of the ball park over the left field wall."

For fifteen seasons, from 1973 through 1987, Mike averaged 36 home runs, 109 RBIs, and 99 walks a season. He also established himself as one of the greatest third basemen of all time, winning eleven Gold Gloves. Mike is eligible to be voted into the Hall of Fame in 1995, and many writers and baseball people expect him to go in on the first ballot.

"Mike Schmidt is definitely a first-ballot entry into the Hall of Fame," says New York sportswriter Jim O'Toole. "I mean, he was one of the greatest of all time and probably the greatest third baseman to have ever played the game."

Mike spent much of the 1988 season somewhere unfamiliar—on the disabled list. He needed surgery for a rotator cuff problem. Mike spent most of his career healthy. This injury took away almost half a season, and with Mike already well into his thirties, it could have marked the beginning of the end.

Mike belted five home runs for the month of April in 1989 and appeared to be on the road back. But when his average fell to .203 in May, he announced his retirement.

Mike could have played out the season and padded his already impressive statistics, but that was not his style. If he could not perform to the best of his abilities, he did not want to keep playing. In a sense, he retired because he refused to let the fans down.

Mike said farewell to his fans at a packed press conference. As he began to recall his earlier days and his accomplishments along the way, he broke down and began to cry. It was hard to say good-bye.

The fans voted him into the all-star game for the twelfth and final time despite his retirement, but Mike did not play.

During his playing career Mike accumulated eight home run crowns and led the National League in slugging five times, in runs batted in four times, and in walks four times. He was the recipient of three Most Valuable Player awards, one World Series MVP award, and eleven Gold Gloves. He also has the dubious honor of owning the third highest strikeout total in major-league history. Mike also served as Philadelphia's team captain from 1978 to 1989.

These days, Mike lives with his wife and two children in suburban Philadelphia, where he participates in the Philadelphia Child Guidance Clinic and other charities. Mike was always involved in charitable work during his playing days, and now he has much more time to devote to it. Mike's hobbies include collecting toy trains and playing golf. In the back of his mind, he waits for a cold January day when his phone will ring with the news that he has been elected to the baseball Hall of Fame.

Schmidt, Michael Jack
b. Sept. 27, 1949, Dayton, Ohio.

YEAR	TEAM	GAMES	BA	SA	AB	H	2B	3B
1972	PHI N	13	.206	.294	34	7	0	0
1973		132	.196	.373	367	72	11	0
1974		162	.282	.546	568	160	28	0
1975		158	.249	.523	562	140	34	3
1976		160	.262	.524	584	153	31	4
1977		154	.274	.574	544	149	27	11
1978		145	.251	.435	513	129	27	2
1979		160	.253	.564	541	137	25	4
1980		150	.286	.624	548	157	25	8
1981		102	.316	.644	354	112	19	2
1982		148	.280	.547	514	144	26	3
1983		154	.255	.524	534	136	16	4
1984		151	.277	.536	528	146	23	3
1985		158	.277	.532	549	152	31	5
1986		160	.290	.547	552	160	29	1
1987		147	.293	.548	522	153	28	0
1988		108	.249	.405	390	97	21	2
1989		42	.203	.372	148	30	7	0
18 yrs.		2404	.267	.527	8352	2234	408	59

DIVISIONAL PLAYOFF SERIES

YEAR	TEAM	GAMES	BA	SA	AB	H	2B	3B
1981	PHI N	5	.250	.500	16	4	1	0

LEAGUE CHAMPIONSHIP SERIES

YEAR	TEAM	GAMES	BA	SA	AB	H	2B	3B
1976	PHI N	3	.308	.462	13	4	2	0
1977		4	.063	.063	16	1	0	0
1978		4	.200	.333	15	3	2	0
1980		5	.208	.250	24	5	1	0
1983		4	.467	.800	15	7	2	0
5 yrs.		20	.241	.361	83	20	7	0

WORLD SERIES

YEAR	TEAM	GAMES	BA	SA	AB	H	2B	3B
1980	PHI N	6	.381	.714	21	8	1	0
1983		5	.050	.050	20	1	0	0
2 yrs.		11	.220	.390	41	9	1	0

YEAR	HR	HR%	R	RBI	BB	SO	SB
1972	0	2.9	2	3	5	15	0
1973	18	4.9	43	52	62	136	8
1974	36	6.3	108	116	106	138	23
1975	38	6.8	93	95	101	180	29
1976	38	6.5	112	107	100	149	14
1977	38	7.0	114	101	104	122	15
1978	21	4.1	93	78	91	103	19
1979	45	8.3	109	114	120	115	9
1980	48	8.8	104	121	89	119	12
1981	31	8.8	78	91	73	71	12
1982	34	6.8	108	87	107	131	14
1983	40	7.5	104	109	128	148	7
1984	36	6.8	93	106	92	116	5
1985	33	6.0	89	93	87	117	1
1986	37	6.7	97	119	89	84	1
1987	35	6.7	88	113	83	80	2
1988	12	3.1	52	62	49	42	3
1989	6	4.1	19	28	21	17	0
18 yrs.	548	6.6	1506	1595	1507	1883	174
	7th	8th				3rd	

DIVISIONAL PLAYOFF SERIES

YEAR	HR	HR%	R	RBI	BB	SO	SB
1981	0	6.3	3	2	4	2	0

LEAGUE CHAMPIONSHIP SERIES

YEAR	HR	HR%	R	RBI	BB	SO	SB
1976	0	0.0	1	2	0	1	0
1977	0	0.0	2	1	2	3	0
1978	0	0.0	1	1	2	2	0
1980	0	0.0	1	1	1	6	1
1983	1	6.7	5	2	2	3	0
5 yrs.	1	1.2	10	7	7	15	1

WORLD SERIES

YEAR	HR	HR%	R	RBI	BB	SO	SB
1980	2	9.5	6	7	4	3	0
1983	0	0.0	0	0	0	6	0
2 yrs.	2	4.9	6	7	4	9	0

CHAPTER TEN

Bob Horner

When Bob Horner was playing baseball at Arizona State University, it seemed that he was destined for greatness. Horner, with his six-foot–one-inch, 195-pound frame, was a prime candidate for the big leagues—Arizona State seemed to just pump out major-league all-stars at will. Reggie Jackson, Rick Monday, and Sal Bando all played ball at Arizona State. Even Horner's college teammate, shortstop Hubie Brooks, became an all-star player.

Robert Horner was born in Junction City, Kansas, but his family moved to California before Bob was two. He began playing baseball with his father, Jim, at the tender age of four and immediately dreamed of being a big leaguer.

"I realized I wanted to be a major leaguer a long time ago—as soon as I started playing baseball," he said. "When I turned on the television set and saw those guys out there, I wanted to be out there too. I think that's the childhood dream of every boy."

The family settled in Phoenix, Arizona, in 1972. Bob began belting home runs as the star of his Little League team. His father was not only the coach but his personal mentor, often working with Bob on the mental approach to hitting and dealing with batting slumps.

Horner played shortstop in high school, and by his senior year he was attracting scouts. The Oakland Athletics drafted Bob in the fifteenth round of the 1975 draft. But the A's were not offering a lot of money, and Bob wanted a college education. He turned down the A's offer and decided to attend Arizona State in the fall of 1975.

"By my sophomore year in college, when I made All-American, I began to think that I would get drafted pretty high and that I would have a pretty good chance to make the major leagues," Bob said.

The power-hitting Horner was heavily scouted at Arizona State, and the Atlanta Braves made no secret about wanting to sign him.

"We need a third baseman with power," commented Atlanta's director of player personnel, Bill Lucas. "Horner not only has power but he's got 'way over the fence' power."

Bob dominated college ball during his junior year as he and Hubie Brooks led the Sun Devils to the College World Series. Bob smashed 25 home runs and drove in 98 runs in only 57 games.

Horner was the first player chosen in the 1978 amateur draft. The Atlanta Braves couldn't wait to pencil him in as their starting third baseman. For Bob, it seemed as if his childhood dream was finally coming true.

"I'm excited because I was picked first and because Atlanta's ballpark is a hitter's paradise," Horner said on the day of the draft.

It seemed a match made in heaven—the big, burly home run hitter playing 81 home games a season at the "Launching Pad," the nickname affectionately given to Atlanta's Fulton County Stadium by power hitters who liked the dimensions. The fence was only 6 feet high and 330 feet deep down the lines.

Bob skipped his senior year in college and was scheduled to report to the Braves' AA minor-league team in Savannah, Georgia. But he convinced Lucas that he was ready for the pros. He reported to the Braves on June 16, 1978, and made an immediate impact, belting his first major-league home run in his first game.

Other ballplayers have gone directly from college to the pros, but they often struggle for a few years before reaching stardom. Two examples are Hall of Fame pitcher Sandy Koufax and all-star outfielder Dick Groat.

Bob became an instant star with the Braves. He won the Rookie of the Year award after hitting 23 home runs and driving in 63 runs in only 89 games. He became the only player ever to win the College Player of the Year and the major-league rookie honors in the same year. Bob and his sweet swing were impressing just about everyone in the league.

"I'm amazed at how well he's been able to adjust to the big leagues with no minor league experience," said former Philadelphia relief ace Tug McGraw. "Bob Horner has done as good a job as any new major league player I've seen—whether he came from college or the minors."

The comparisons to former Braves Hall of Fame sluggers Hank Aaron and Eddie Mathews were inevitable. Horner seemed bound to accomplish great things on the baseball field.

Then health problems and contract squabbles began to steal some of the luster from his star. Bob had minor shoulder surgery after his rookie campaign, and then a small bone chip in his ankle forced him to miss the first month of the 1979 season. Meanwhile, a bitter contract battle was taking place between the young slugger and Braves owner Ted Turner.

During his rookie season, Bob was paid the minimum wage for rookies, 21,000 dollars. However, with incentives and bonuses, he actually made close to 180,000 dollars. His contract was not specific about exactly what was salary and what was incentive money. So when the Braves offered the young slugger 100,000 dollars for the next season, Horner's agent, Bucky Woy, claimed that Bob was due at least 146,000 dollars, which he said allowed for the maximum 20 percent pay cut that the Braves could implement.

The battles between Horner and the Atlanta management were waged in the media. In a poll taken during the contract dispute, 95 percent of Atlantans sided with Turner and the Braves management.

Bob was also causing a lot of resentment from older players who felt that his contract demands were unreasonable. New York Mets star outfielder Lee Mazzilli was quite vocal about the whole affair. "There are guys who have played 8–10 years, who have put in their dues, who aren't making the money he is now.

For a man to play three months and make $146,000, that's a lot of money. It's more than I make."

When the case went to a baseball arbitrator to decide, Woy insisted that Horner be made a free agent, meaning he could sign a contract with the highest-bidding team. The arbitrator ultimately ruled in favor of the 146,000-dollar salary, but decided that the Braves still retained all rights to the young slugger.

Horner and his home-run swing returned to action and he was accepted as a true superstar. In spite of missing the first month of the 1979 season, Bob batted .314, belted 33 homers, and drove in 98 runs in only 121 games.

Bob reported to spring training early in 1980 intent on improving his defensive skills at third base and first base. Nobody seemed too concerned with his fielding, though. It was his bat that was drawing accolades.

"Bob Horner can break any home-run record he wants to if he stays healthy and plays in enough games," home-run champion Hank Aaron said that spring. "He was born to hit a baseball."

Unfortunately, Bob began the 1980 season very slowly, hitting only .059 with six errors after ten games during Atlanta's dismal 1–9 start. Turner, perhaps remembering Horner's contract stance, which to him seemed arrogant, decided to send the young slugger to the minor leagues. Bob felt slighted by the demotion. He refused to report to the Braves' AAA affiliate at Richmond, Virginia, and demanded to be traded.

Turner retreated after a ten-day stalemate, and Horner returned to Atlanta, where he sat on the bench. The clashing personalities of Horner and Turner probably hurt Bob's career more than people think. His heart was not in it anymore.

"Physically, I'm back, but I can't tell you where my mind is. This situation hurt me and humiliated me. Ted Turner made his point and I just want to get out of his way," he said.

Bob was eventually received back by his teammates, but the media and the fans were lukewarm.

"My reception? I felt welcome but nothing spectacular," he said after being reinstated.

Bob stayed with the Braves and enjoyed some fine seasons, but he was never fully accepted by Turner as a member of the team. Even after he became field captain, there was always a trade rumor floating around with Bob's name involved.

Bob enjoyed some fine offensive seasons during the next few years. He teamed with center fielder Dale Murphy to form one of the most potent home run combinations in baseball. In 1982 the duo led the Braves to their first division championship in fourteen years. The Braves lost the pennant that year to the St. Louis Cardinals.

In 1984, chronic shoulder problems and a broken wrist allowed Bob to play only 32 games. Some doubted whether he would ever be able to play again.

He worked hard on his rehabilitation to come back and regain his home-run stroke. Limited to 130 games in 1985, Bob still smashed 27 round-trippers with 89 RBIs. Even so, the Braves suffered another dismal season.

Still, Bob gained a place in the record books. On July 6, 1986, he became the ninth player in modern baseball history to hit four home runs in a game.

Bob victimized the visiting Montreal Expos, but despite his brilliant display of power, the Braves dropped the game 11–8. You could say it was Bob's professional career in a nutshell: terrific statistics and personal stardom, yet ultimately disappointing results.

Bob hit solo homers in the second and fourth innings against Montreal starter Andy McGaffigan. He added a three-run home run against McGaffigan in the fifth inning and hit a solo shot against all-star reliever Jeff Reardon in the ninth. The Atlanta fans gave Horner a five-minute standing ovation as he rounded the bases the last time.

"In my wildest dreams I would never have expected to do anything like that," a smiling Horner said after the game. "It's just one of those things that happen and you can't explain it."

Bob finished the 1986 season with 27 home runs and 87 runs batted in while posting a .273 batting average. He played out his option with the Braves and became a free agent. His stormy relationship with Ted Turner was finally over, but other teams were reluctant to sign him. His history of injuries, and perhaps a reputation as a troublemaker due to his contract squabbles, overshadowed his accomplishments at the plate. Bob signed a contract with the Yakult Swallows of the Japanese League. He led the league in home runs and then returned to the United States, signing a one-year contract with the St. Louis Cardinals for 1988.

"I was offered more money to stay in Japan," Horner said. "But I'm satisfied and happy to be back in the States playing ball. It's what I wanted to do."

Horner's swing, so accustomed to Atlanta's Fulton County Stadium, had a hard time adjusting to St. Louis's cavernous Busch Stadium, which is tailored to speedy teams and where home runs are hard to come by. Injuries once again took their toll, and Horner retired after hitting only three homers in 60 games for the Redbirds.

He finished his ten-year career with 218 lifetime home runs in only 1,020 games, a .277 average, and 685 runs batted in. It was a career filled with glowing accomplishments and accolades, but also with the disappointment of unfulfilled potential. Bob Horner had dreamed of a major-league career, and was supposed to be the next Hank Aaron or at least the next Eddie Mathews. He was neither. Instead, injuries, contract disputes, and head-to-head collisions with one of baseball's strong-headed owners combined to make Bob Horner's career fall short of his dreams.

Horner, James Robert
b. Aug. 6, 1957, Junction City, Kans.

YEAR	TEAM	GAMES	BA	SA	AB	H	2B	3B
1978	ATL N	89	.266	.539	323	86	17	1
1979		121	.314	.552	487	153	15	1
1980		124	.268	.529	463	124	14	1
1981		79	.277	.460	300	83	10	0
1982		140	.261	.501	499	130	24	0
1983		104	.303	.528	386	117	25	1
1984		32	.274	.425	113	31	8	0
1985		130	.267	.499	483	129	25	3
1986		141	.273	.472	517	141	22	0
1988	STL N	60	.257	.354	206	53	9	1
10 yrs.		1020	.277	.499	3777	1047	169	8

LEAGUE CHAMPIONSHIP SERIES

1982	ATL N	3	.091	.091	11	1	0	0

YEAR	HR	HR%	R	RBI	BB	SO	SB
1978	23	7.1	50	63	24	42	0
1979	33	6.8	66	98	22	74	0
1980	35	7.6	81	89	27	50	3
1981	15	5.0	42	42	32	39	2
1982	32	6.4	85	97	66	75	3
1983	20	5.2	75	68	50	63	4
1984	3	2.7	15	19	14	17	0
1985	27	5.6	61	89	50	57	1
1986	27	5.2	70	87	52	72	1
1988	3	1.5	15	33	32	23	0
10 yrs.	218	5.8	560	685	369	512	14

LEAGUE CHAMPIONSHIP SERIES

YEAR	HR	HR%	R	RBI	BB	SO	SB
1982	0	0.0	0	0	0	2	0

CHAPTER ELEVEN

Mark Whiten

Mark Whiten's lethal weapon was already known throughout the major leagues as one of the best. Armed with one of the strongest and most accurate throwing arms in the history of baseball, the six-foot–three-inch, 215-pound Whiten had already made his mark defensively. It was his batting that people were worried about and, at the tender age of twenty-six, he found himself with his third major-league team.

Born on November 25, 1966, in the warm, sunny Florida city of Pensacola, Mark was able to play baseball year-round. The practice paid off. He became the star player at Pensacola High School, and earned Most Valuable Player honors at Pensacola Junior College.

In the 1986 January amateur draft, the Toronto Blue Jays

drafted Whiten in the fifth round. He was assigned to Medicine Hat, where he began the climb to the major leagues. Whiten showed flashes of brilliance at Medicine Hat and was nicknamed Hard-hittin' Whiten after collecting 10 homers in an abbreviated season.

By his third season in the minors, Whiten and his lethal-weapon throwing arm were getting all the attention, while his bat was steady but unspectacular.

"He's got a cannon for an arm," said Mark's Class A manager, Doug Ault. "He might have the strongest arm in the minors and the majors right now."

Whiten kept improving his game and was even ranked by *Baseball America* as the number-one prospect in the Triple A International League after batting .290 for the Syracuse Chiefs in 1990. Still, though he was built like the typical power hitter, he was not hitting a lot of home runs.

Mark's first taste of the big leagues came on July 12, 1990, when he was called up to the Blue Jays to replace injured outfielder Glenallen Hill, who had injured his toes while sleepwalking in his home.

Mark filled in adequately for Hill, compiling a .270 batting average in one month. His first major-league home run was a solo shot against Kansas City pitcher Kevin Appier on July 26.

Whiten was sent back down to Syracuse on August 13, but his hot bat and strong arm merited another call up on August 30. This time, Mark was up for good.

The 1991 season began slowly for Mark, and he was soon traded with Hill by the pitching-hungry Blue Jays to the Cleveland Indians for pitcher Tom Candiotti. Although he was disappointed at first, the trade proved to be good for Whiten, who could now play more regularly than he had with powerhouse Toronto.

Mark was considered to have the best throwing arm in the American League during his two seasons with the often inept Cleveland Indians. Still, Mark's offensive numbers were not impressive. During the 1992 campaign he belted only 9 homers in over 500 at bats.

Mark was acquired by the St. Louis Cardinals during the off-season and viewed spring training as an almost do-or-die situation. No longer a rookie, he was running out of chances to prove himself.

So when Mark donned his St. Louis Cardinal uniform in 1993, he decided to change his batting style. He abandoned the spread-legged, wide stance he had used in the past and adopted a more conventional even stance. The simple change worked.

That season Mark established himself as one of the new premier power hitters in baseball. His awesome power and run production helped lead the Cardinals to a second-place finish.

"I've always felt that I had the strength to hit home runs," Mark said. "It was frustrating when I didn't. You look at a guy my size, and you expect power. When I didn't show it, people couldn't understand why. It just took time to learn."

While the Cardinals spent the summer closely chasing the front-running Philadelphia Phillies, Whiten was impressing everyone with his eye-popping throws and newfound power.

He put on a spectacular display on August 11 when he became the first visiting player in Pittsburgh's Three Rivers Stadium history to hit a home run into the right-field upper deck.

The only other players to reach the upper deck since 1970 were Willie Stargell and Bobby Bonilla.

Then, to cap off a wonderful season, Mark joined the record books on September 7, 1993, when he belted four home runs during the second game of a doubleheader against the home-town Cincinnati Reds.

Whiten's record-tying 12-RBI game led the Cards to a 15–2 nightcap victory during an incredible night for offensive production. The Reds took the opener 14–13 in a slug fest. Mark drove in one run during the first game, giving him 13 for the doubleheader, tying a National League record.

Mark hit a first-inning grand slam off of Cincinnati starter Tim Leubbers and 2 three-run homers off of Scott Anderson in the sixth and seventh innings before belting a ninth-inning two-run homer against Rob Dibble.

After the game Mark was greeted with a hero's welcome by all of his teammates. They held their bats in the air, saluting the young slugger.

"It's nice to have attention now and then," the humble Whiten said. "I've never had a game like this. It's like when Michael Jordan gets in that 'zone', he knows he's going to score 50 points. That's kind of the way it felt for me."

Mark finished the season strongly and gave the contending Cardinals hope for the future by establishing himself as a rising star. His teammates are looking forward to seeing his progress.

"He can put up numbers with anybody," said St. Louis first baseman Gregg Jefferies. "I know he can hit 25 home runs and drive in 100 runs every year. He can steal a lot of bases, too. He hasn't been playing at this level that long. Just wait."

Yes, just wait.

Whiten, Mark Anthony

b. Nov. 25, 1966, Pensacola, Fla.

YEAR	TEAM	GAMES	BA	SA	AB	H	2B	3B
1990	TOR A	33	.273	.375	88	24	1	1
1991	2 teams TOR A (46G—.221) CLE A (70G—.256)							
"	total	116	.243	.388	407	99	18	7
1992	CLE A	148	.254	.360	508	129	19	4
3 yrs.		297	.251	.373	1003	252	38	12

YEAR	HR	HR%	R	RBI	BB	SO	SB
1990	2	2.3	12	7	7	14	2
1991	9	2.2	46	45	30	85	4
1992	9	1.8	73	43	72	102	16
3 yrs.	20	2.0	131	95	109	201	72

Epilogue

While the rules of baseball have stayed pretty much the same for more than a century, strategies and styles of play have changed dramatically over the years.

With artificial turf and large domed stadiums making home runs more difficult to hit, the emphasis in today's game is on team speed and defense. The game is now dominated by the infield hit, the stolen base, the hit-and-run, and speedy outfielders who track down long shots in the power alleys. The 1992 baseball season was a perfect example of this: The Pittsburgh Pirates and Montreal Expos ran first and second in the National League's Eastern Division, yet both clubs were near the bottom third in the home run department. In a sense this takes the game back to the premodern era, before Babe Ruth revolutionized the home run into an offensive weapon.

Of course, home runs are still being hit and sluggers are still in demand. The World Champion Toronto Blue Jays and the Western Division–Champion Oakland A's were both near the top of the major leagues in the home-run categories for 1992. And what fan doesn't stop to watch Cecil Fielder, Mark McGwire, Barry Bonds, Jose Canseco, or Mark Whiten step into the batter's box? Baseball fans have always had a love affair with the home run, and ever since Lou Gehrig made baseball history by hitting the first four home-run game in the modern era, the four home-run game has ranked as one of the most exciting events in all of sports.

Prime candidates to hit four round-trippers in a game can be found in both leagues. The American League's Detroit Tigers listed Cecil Fielder, Mickey Tettleton, and Rob Deer in their 1992 lineups. All three sluggers belt home runs with ferocity and great distance. According to the IBM Tale of the Tape, all three averaged better than 392 feet a home run for 1992—far enough to hit a ball out of almost any park in the league. The National League can boast former MVP Barry Bonds, Matt Williams, and Fred McGriff, all of whom hit for high average as well as outstanding home-run totals.

However, many of today's top hitters aren't as consistent as the steadier players of yesterday: Fielder, Tettleton, and Deer may hit the ball hard and far, but they each have a record of striking out more than a 100 times per year.

Veteran baseball broadcaster and Hall of Fame outfielder Ralph Kiner has seen the game change from players who hit for average to today's sluggers, who simply swing from their heels.

Even though Kiner admits there are several players who are capable of hitting four runs in a game, he believes the odds are against this happening. "The potential hitter today strikes out much too often," he says. "They are swinging too hard."

Kiner's point is well-taken. Logic dictates that the next player to hit four home runs in a game won't merely be a slugger, but also an accomplished, disciplined hitter like Lou Gehrig, Willie Mays, and Chuck Klein.

On the other hand, logic can sometimes be thrown out the window.

"Anything can happen in the game today," says veteran New York sportswriter Jim O'Toole. "With the way these guys swing and the harder the pitchers throw, anything can happen. You'll probably get some nondescript guy, averaging twenty homers a year, come around and do it next."

Mark Whiten's 1993 home run feat backs up O'Toole's philosophy. Before adjusting his stance, Whiten certainly fit O'Toole's description.

Who knows what will happen when a batter steps up, swings his bat, and tries to whack one out. In the end, when the hitter digs in and the pitcher winds up, statistics and predictions become meaningless. As Pat Seerey reminds us, sometimes all it takes is a little luck to hit four homers in a game. Luck and home-run power.

Bibliography

The following sources were used in research for this book:

BOOKS

Adler, Bill. *Baseball Wit.* New York: Crown, 1986.

Anderson, Dave, Murray Chass, Robert Creamer, and Harold Rosenthal. *The Yankees.* New York: Random House, 1979.

Bilovsky, Frank, and Richard Wescott. *The Phillies' Encyclopedia.* Philadelphia: Leisure Press, 1st edition, 1984.

Egan, Terry, Stan Friedman, and Mike Levine. *The Macmillan Book of Baseball Stories.* New York: Macmillan USA, 1992.

Hubler, Richard G. *Lou Gehrig: The Iron Horse of Baseball.* Boston: Houghton Mifflin, 1941.

Jennison, Christopher. *Wait Till Next Year.* New York: Norton Books, 1974.

Peary, Jim. *Cult Baseball Players.* New York: Fireside Books, 1968.

Rust Jr., Art. *Legends.* New York: McGraw-Hill, 1989.

Shatzin, Mike. *The Ballplayers.* New York: Arbor House, 1990.

Wright, Jim. *Mike Schmidt.* New York: GP Putnam & Sons, NY, 1979.

MAGAZINES

Atlanta Braves Banner, 1983
Atlanta Braves Scorebook 1979,
   Volume 14, #3
Atlanta Braves Scorebook 1980,
   Volume 15, #4
Beckett Baseball Magazine, August
   1991

Cleveland Indians 1993 Media
   Guide
Sports Illustrated, July 14, 1986
Street & Smith's Baseball Yearbook,
   1987
Toronto Blue Jays 1991 Media
   Guide

NEWSPAPER ARTICLES

New York Times:
June 4, 1932
July 11, 1936
July 5, 1939
June 3, 1941
September 1, 1950
August 1, 1954
August 2, 1954
March 29, 1958
May 1, 1961
April 3, 1972
April 4, 1972
May 14, 1972
April 18, 1976
May 16, 1978
January 24, 1979
June 5, 1979
April 23, 1980
April 28, 1980
July 7, 1986

April 19, 1987
January 15, 1988

New York Daily News:
January 24, 1979

Associated Press:
April 23, 1980
April 26, 1980
August 12, 1993
September 8, 1993

United Press International:
June 5, 1979

New York-Telegram:
July 14, 1945

Sporting News:
May 14, 1947
July 26, 1948

September 5, 1950
June 17, 1959
September 3, 1978
December 9, 1978
March 31, 1979
April 21, 1979
May 17, 1980
April 24, 1982
October 4, 1982
November 29, 1982
December 20, 1982
October 27, 1986

Cleveland Plain-Dealer:
January 11, 1970
February 19, 1974

Cleveland News:
December 29, 1944
June 3, 1948

St. Louis Post-Dispatch:
July 18, 1979

Miscellaneous

Press releases from various teams
National Baseball Hall of Fame Library and Archive, Cooperstown, New York (All the sources provided by the Hall of Fame Library are listed separately above.)
The Hall of Fame Library also assisted by providing files on Pat Seerey and Bob Horner.

Index

A Let's-Read-and-Find-Out Book™

Sunshine Makes the Seasons

REVISED EDITION

by Franklyn M. Branley · illustrated by Giulio Maestro

A Harper Trophy Book · Harper & Row, Publishers

LET'S READ-AND-FIND-OUT BOOK CLUB EDITION

The *Let's-Read-and-Find-Out Book*™ series was originated by Dr. Franklyn M. Branley, Astronomer Emeritus and former Chairman of the American Museum–Hayden Planetarium, and was formerly co-edited by him and Dr. Roma Gans, Professor Emeritus of Childhood Education, Teachers College, Columbia University. Text and illustrations are checked for accuracy by an expert in the relevant field.

Library of Congress Cataloging in Publication Data
Branley, Franklyn Mansfield, 1915–
   Sunshine makes the seasons.

  (Let's-read-and-find-out science book)
  Summary: Describes how sunshine and the tilt of the
earth's axis are responsible for the changing seasons.
    1. Seasons—Juvenile literature.   2. Sunshine—Juvenile
literature. [1. Seasons] I. Maestro, Giulio, ill.
II. Title.   III. Series.
QB631.B73 1985b   525'.5   85-47540
ISBN 0-690-04481-X
ISBN 0-690-04482-8 (lib. bdg.)

  (A Let's-read-and-find-out book)
  "A Harper trophy book."
ISBN 0-06-445019-8 (pbk.)   85-42750

Sunshine warms the earth.

If the sun stopped shining, the earth would get colder and colder. We would freeze. The whole earth would freeze.

The sun shines all through the year. But we are warmer in summer than in winter. The amount of sunshine makes the difference.

The earth spins around, or rotates, once in twenty-four hours. That's why we have day and night. When we are on the sun side of the earth, there is daylight. As the earth rotates, we turn away from the sun. There is sunset and then night.

At the same time that the earth spins, it goes around the sun. The earth takes a year to make one trip around the sun.

During a year the length of our day changes. In winter the days are short. It may be dark by the time you get home from school. It is cold because we don't get many hours of sunshine.

As we move into spring, days become a bit longer. By summer they are even longer.

The days may be so long that it is still light when you go to bed. It is warm because we get many hours of sunshine.

After the long days of summer, the days begin to get shorter and cooler. It is fall and time to go back to school.

All through the year the earth has been rotating once in twenty-four hours, giving us day and night. And all through the year the lengths of darkness and daylight have been changing. The seasons have been changing too.

You can see the reason for these changes by using an orange for the earth, a pencil, and a flashlight. Push a pencil through an orange from top to bottom. The top is the North Pole. You can mark it with an N. The bottom is the South Pole. Using a marking pen, draw a line around the orange halfway between the poles. That's the equator. Stick a pin in the orange about halfway between the equator and the North Pole. Imagine this is where you live.

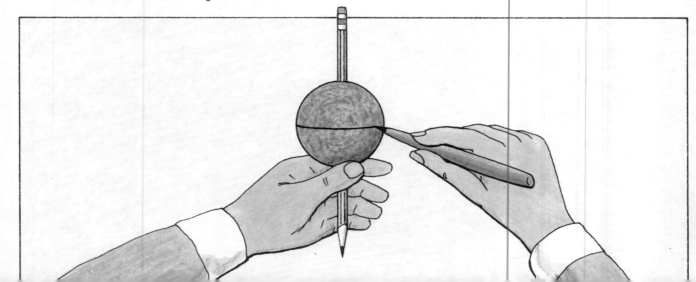

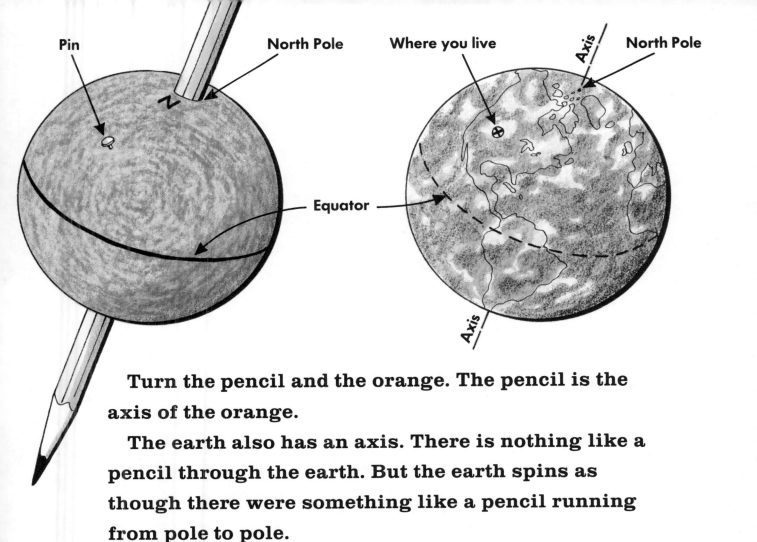

Turn the pencil and the orange. The pencil is the axis of the orange.

The earth also has an axis. There is nothing like a pencil through the earth. But the earth spins as though there were something like a pencil running from pole to pole.

13

Hold the axis of the orange straight up and down. In a darkened room, have someone shine a flashlight on the orange.

The light is supposed to be the sun. The part of the orange toward the flashlight is in daylight. The other half is in darkness.

Daylight falls on the North Pole and also the South Pole, even when you spin the orange.

Walk all around the flashlight. Keep the light shining on the orange. That would be the same as the earth going all around the sun. It would be a year. Keep the axis straight up and down.

Wherever you are as you circle the flashlight, the orange is lighted from pole to pole. All through the year and all over the earth, days and nights would be the same length. There would be no change in seasons.

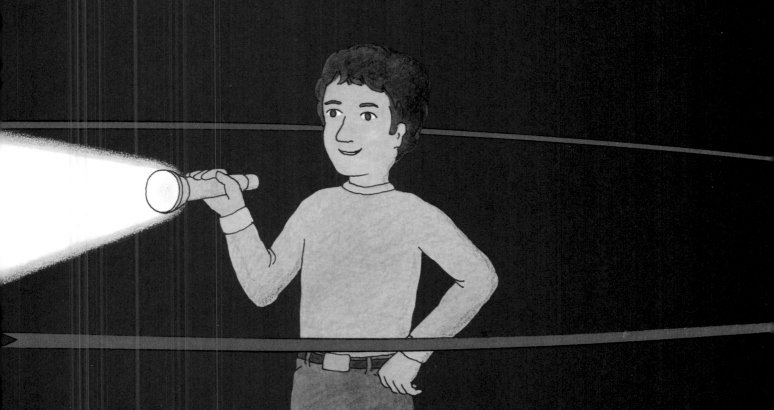

But we know that does not happen on the earth. The days get shorter and then longer as the earth goes around the sun. And winter changes to summer. It's because the axis of the earth is not straight up and down. It is tilted.

Let's experiment with the orange. This time tilt the axis the way it is tilted in the picture. That's the way the earth's axis is tilted. Hold the orange so the North Pole is tilted away from the flashlight.

Turn the orange all the way around, and you will see that the pin is in the light only a short time. The northern half of the earth has short days and long nights. Sunlight does not fall on the North Pole. The North Pole has its long winter night. It is winter and it is cold.

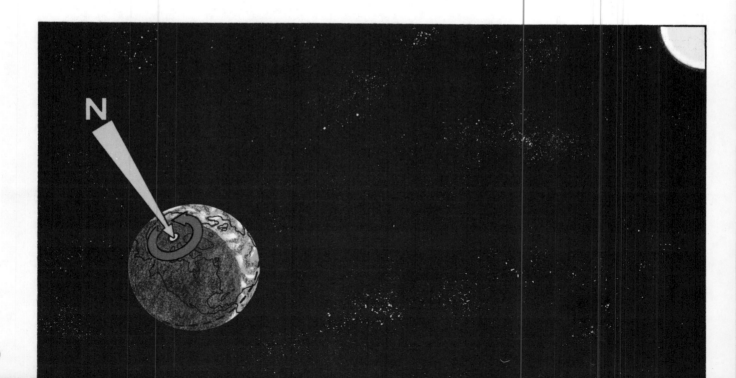

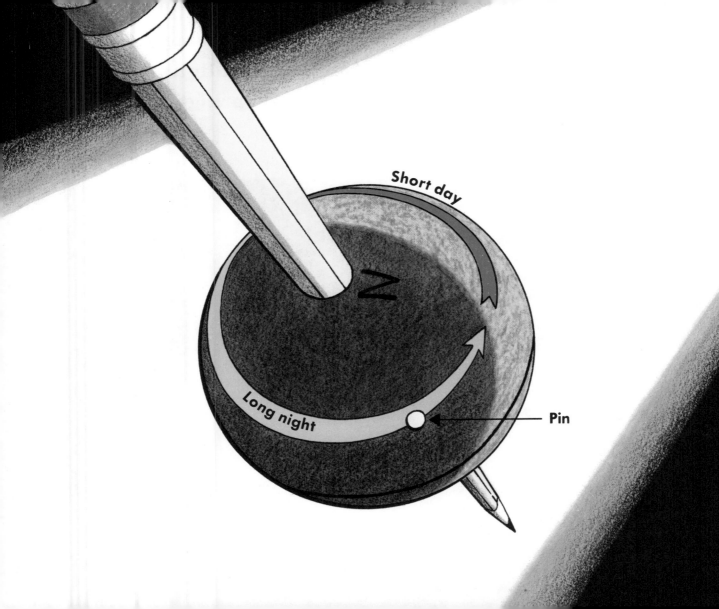

Keep the axis of the orange tilted in the same direction and go partway around the flashlight. Now the light falls on both poles. It is springtime in the north. Days are getting longer.

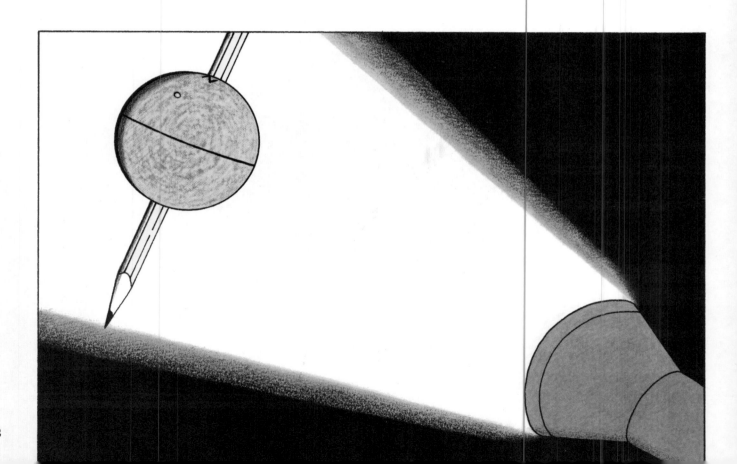

Without changing the tilt of the axis, move until
you are halfway around the flashlight from where
you started. Soon the North Pole will be tilted
toward the light. It is summer.

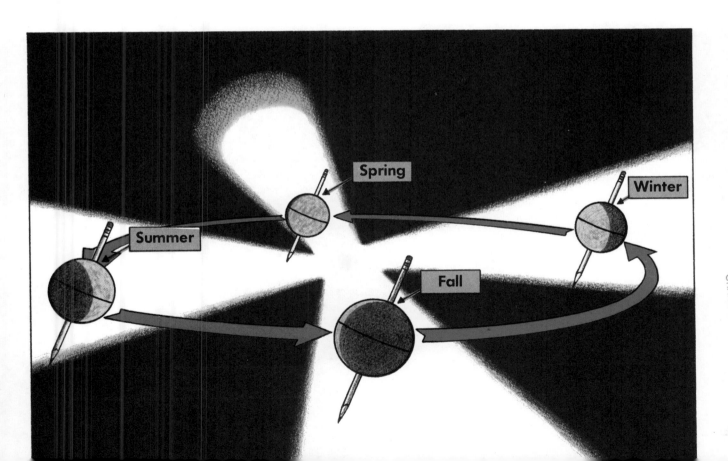

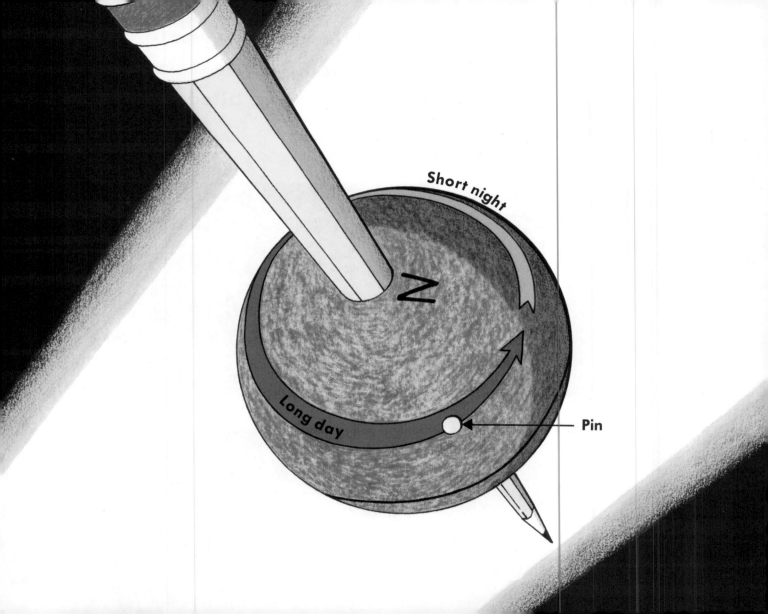

As you turn the orange, the pin is in the light longer than it is in the dark. The northern half of the earth has long days and short nights. The North Pole has its long summer day. It is summer and it is warm.

Keep moving around the flashlight. Remember, always keep the orange tilted in the same direction. You'll see that once again light falls on both the North Pole and the South Pole of the orange. It is fall in the north. The days are getting shorter, and cooler too.

Keep moving around and you come back to winter.

Winter   Spring   Summer   Fall

They happen because sunshine makes the seasons, and because the axis of the earth is tilted.

Axis

The southern half of the earth has seasons too. They are the opposites of our seasons. When it is summer and we are going to the beach, people on the southern half of the earth have winter. They are skating and skiing.

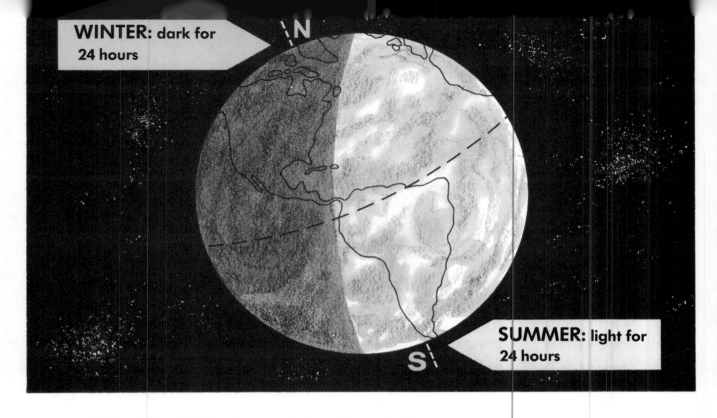

WINTER: dark for 24 hours

SUMMER: light for 24 hours

The North Pole and the South Pole also have seasons. Their winters are cold and dark. The sun does not rise every day. It is dark all winter long.

During summer at the poles, the sun does not set every day. For several weeks there is no night.

Seasons at the Poles are opposite. When the North Pole has winter, the South Pole has summer. Six months later, when it is winter at the South Pole, it is summer at the North Pole.

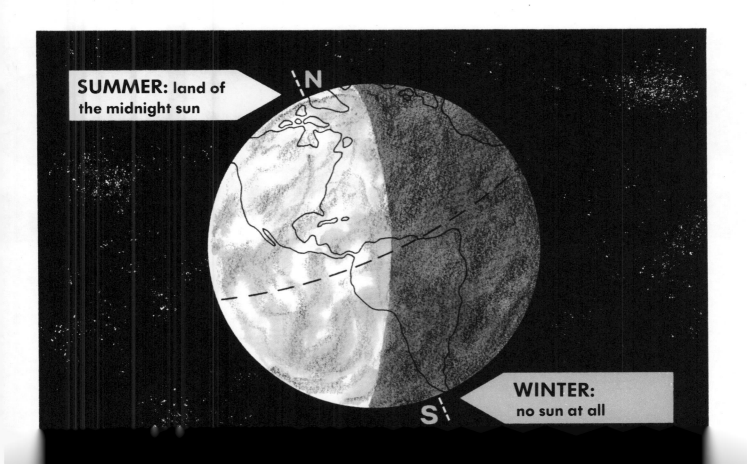

SUMMER: land of the midnight sun

N

S

WINTER: no sun at all

Along the equator it is warm all the time. The temperature stays about the same all through the year. You can see why if you experiment with the orange. Move the pin to the equator.

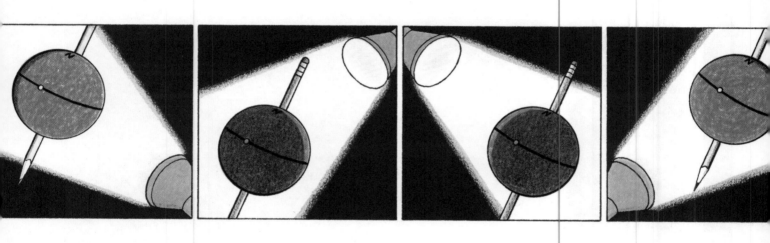

Watch the pin to see what happens as you go through a year. You'll see that day and night are just about the same length in summer and winter, spring and fall.

That's good if you like warm weather all the time. But it's also nice to see snow once in a while, to see the flowers and birds of springtime, to go swimming in summer, and have pumpkins in the fall.

Year after year the days change, and so do the
seasons. We have winter, spring, summer, and fall
because the sun warms the earth. And because the
axis of the earth is tilted.

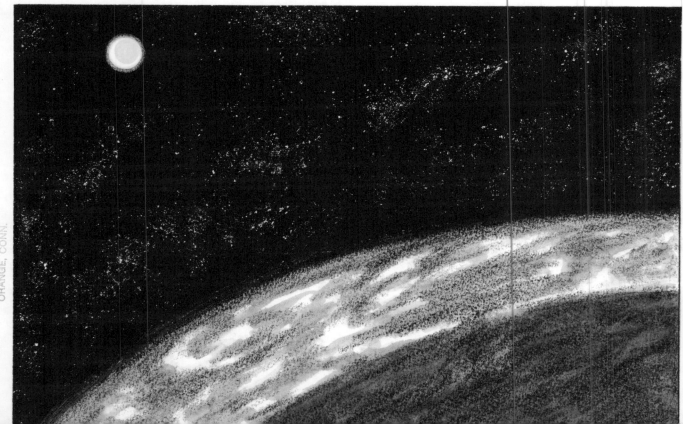